chibi Vampire
The Novel
5

STORY BY TOHRU KAI
ART BY YUNA KAGESAKI

HAMBURG // LONDON // LOS ANGELES // TOKYO

Chibi Vampire: The Novel 5
Written by Tohru Kai
Art by Yuna Kagesaki

Translation - Andrew Cunningham
Design and Layout - Michael Paolilli
Cover Design - Colin Graham
Editor - Michelle Prather
Senior Editor - Jenna Winterberg

Pre-Production Supervisor - Vince Rivera
Digital Imaging Manager - Chris Buford
Art Director - Al-Insan Lashley
Creative Director - Anne Marie Horne
Managing Editor - Vy Nguyen
Editor-in-Chief - Rob Tokar
Publisher - Mike Kiley
President and COO - John Parker
CEO and Chief Creative Officer - Stu Levy

A  Novel

TOKYOPOP Inc.
5900 Wilshire Blvd. Suite 2000
Los Angeles, CA 90036

E-mail: info@TOKYOPOP.com
Come visit us online at www.TOKYOPOP.com

ISBN: 978-1-59816-926-3

First TOKYOPOP printing: July 2008
10 9 8 7 6 5 4 3 2 1
Printed in the USA

CONTENTS

"U-SU-I, GOOD MORNING!" AYAHA BEAMED, BOTH ARMS WRAPPED AROUND KENTA'S NECK.

WHEN AYAHA
TURNED AROUND,
MAKI ASKED, "DO
YOU LOVE USUI?"

"UGH! STOP IT,
MAKI!" KARIN
YELPED, LEAPING
ON HER.

"I DIDN'T MEAN TO— JUUGH!" WITH SHINOBU HOLDING ON TO HER FINGER, KARIN LOST CONTROL AND BURST INTO TEARS.

Ayaha's front wheel struck something hard. Inertia sent her body forward, and her chest hit the handlebars, momentarily knocking the wind out of her. Her tires slipped, causing the frame to lose its balance and leaving her sprawled on the pavement with her bicycle on top of her. She'd hit her left elbow, which made pain shoot up her arm, and she'd skinned her knees on the rain-soaked asphalt.

Ayaha pulled her leg out from under the bicycle and glanced up, finding someone sitting on the ground in front of her. The sheets of rain were reflecting the streetlights, preventing her from making out the person's face, but his white shirt and black pants resembled a school uniform.

"Oww . . ." the boy moaned, holding his back.

Ayaha, who was in just as much pain, felt her body becoming hot with anger. She sat up and yelled, "You're the one who came bolting out from a side street! I could've broken something!"

The boy gazed regretfully at her.

Ayaha's heart instantly clenched. She'd only yelled at him because she'd thought he was *her* again—when he stood up, though, he was nearly six feet tall, and his eyes were thuggishly narrow. She gulped nervously. There was no one else on the street this late, and there were few cars driving through the residential streets.

"Sorry," the boy said. "I didn't have an umbrella and was rushing to get home. Are you hurt?" He bowed his head so politely that it took Ayaha by surprise.

When the boy reached out his hand to help her up, Ayaha relaxed a little. She was afraid to take a stranger's hand, though, so she stood up on her own. As she scanned the boy's uniform, she realized it was from Shiihaba First High School—the same school she attended—so she felt a bit more at ease.

The boy didn't seem offended that Ayaha had declined to take his hand. Instead, he picked up her bicycle for her. "Uh-oh . . . it isn't working," he uttered. His face began to cloud over as he tried to push it toward her.

Surprised, Ayaha silently grabbed her bicycle by the handlebars and tried to push it, but the tires wouldn't turn—the chain was snarled. It would take her fifteen minutes to walk home, and the evening autumn rain showed no signs of clearing. It wasn't raining very hard, but walking home without an umbrella would leave her soaked to the bone.

Ayaha must have twisted her ankle in the fall, as well, because when she put weight on her left leg, it hurt. There was no way she'd be able to make it home carrying a broken bicycle. She considered calling and asking to be picked up, but the school bag that had been in the front basket was missing. It must have flown out when she'd crashed. "My bag!"

"Huh? Oh, it's over there . . ." the boy started to say, but he trailed off in horror.

The bag was sitting in a huge puddle by the side of the road. It had opened during the accident, and its contents had spilled into the muddy water. When Ayaha saw her pearl pink cell phone among her muddied items, she let out a moan of despair. Abandoning her bicycle, she grabbed her phone and pressed the power button several times, but there was no response. It was clearly broken.

Ayaha stood there staring dejectedly at her inoperable phone while the boy pulled her bag out of the puddle.

"Are you okay?" he asked.

"Of course not!" she snapped, unable to hold back her irritation. "My bike's broken and my arm and leg are both hurt, so how am I supposed to get home? And now my phone's broken, so I can't call for someone to pick me up! And it's all your fault!"

Ayaha's outburst was exacerbated by the cold, wet sensation she felt as she snatched the handle of her bag, drenched with muddy water, from the boy. Her blouse was soaked and was sticking to her, there was water in her shoes, and her bag was covered with mud. The pain in her ankle and elbow bothered her more than anything else, though. She was worried that the injuries would prevent her from dancing. Missing merely a few days of ballet class would be incredibly difficult to make up.

If this boy hadn't come hurtling out from the side street, none of this would have happened! Ayaha felt tears starting to well up and wiped them away with her fingers. Hearing someone sighing loudly, she jumped. She couldn't help but remember how sinister the boy had seemed at first. He'd been polite so far, so she felt it was safe to express her anger, but perhaps he really was as scary as he looked.

The boy took a step toward her.

Is he going to hit me? Ayaha's hands shot up to protect her face, but the boy didn't do anything except walk past her and hoist her bicycle into the air, hefting it onto his shoulders.

Turning around, he said, "I'm sorry. I'll carry the bike. So . . . which way?"

Astonished, Ayaha stared at the boy quietly.

He seemed to take her silence the wrong way. "Oh, I'm Kenta Usui—from class 1-D—also at Shiihaba First. I was hurrying home from work, but you don't need to be suspicious." Kenta knew he and Ayaha were in the same school because she was wearing her uniform.

Ayaha couldn't imagine anyone who seemed suspicious readily admitting to being truly shady;

nonetheless, the way Kenta identified himself put her suspicions to rest. "Ayaha Ougimachi—from 2-C. I live this way," she replied, walking ahead.

As she glanced back, Ayaha saw Kenta quietly following her, carrying the bike. He was dragging his right leg behind him a little. She wondered if he was hurt, too. In truth, her emotions were a jangled mess, but she was sure this was merely lingering panic from the crash. She had been pedaling faster than usual, trying to get out of the rain as quickly as possible. She normally would have slowed down before crossing a side street, but not today. Any other day, they never would've crashed. Getting hit by a bicycle was much more likely to cause serious injury than falling off one.

Kenta didn't say anything—he just continued to follow Ayaha, limping.

Ayaha began to regret blaming Kenta so angrily. *Maybe I was a little hard on him.* . . . She glanced back at him again. He was a year younger, but he was at least a half a foot taller than she was. With the exception of his narrow, beady eyes, he wasn't bad looking. He also spoke politely and seemed nice. *Is he a good guy who only looks sinister?*

A face that kept people from understanding one's true nature was a real curse. It reminded Ayaha of the famous ballet *The Nutcracker.* In that story, a prince is turned into a doll designed to open nuts. But the heroine, Clara, likes the doll, even though it's far from beautiful. When the curse is broken and the prince is restored to his original form, he takes Clara on a journey through fairyland. It has to be noted that the heroine was the only character who wasn't fooled by appearances, and who could always see the prince inside the nutcracker doll. *Only the heroine . . .* the phrase resonated in Ayaha's mind, but she still had no idea what to say to Kenta.

Ayaha continued in silence, extremely conscious that Kenta was still behind her. They had arrived at her house when her mouth finally opened. "Here."

The name on the tile-roofed Japanese-style gate was not "Ougimachi" but "Kirioka." Kenta frowned at it.

As she pushed the intercom button, Ayaha explained, "It's my aunt's house. I'm only living here temporarily." Suddenly, her cousin picked up the line. "Ah, Shino? It's me—I'm home."

Nodding, Kenta lowered the bike to the ground, pointing the handles toward Ayaha. "I'd better be off. I really am sorry." He bowed his head, turning to head back out into the rain.

When she saw Kenta dragging his leg again, Ayaha found herself calling after him. "Wait!"

Kenta turned in surprise.

Ayaha was worried that she'd sounded a little too eager, so she rephrased her initial choice of words.

"You don't have an umbrella, right? I'll loan you one. And your leg hurts, doesn't it? You should have that taken care of. Come inside."

"No, I couldn't—it's nothing."

Ayaha thought Kenta would've been happy to receive her invitation; instead, he stood there awkwardly in the rain—completely irritating her. After hearing footsteps, she saw the door open from the inside. Her cousin Shinobu emerged, holding an umbrella.

When Shinobu saw Ayaha and Kenta standing there, his glasses flashed. "Aya! Look at you! And that's Usui—from class D, right?" Shinobu also went to Shiihaba First High. He was in a different class, but in the same grade as Kenta, so it wasn't surprising that Shinobu recognized him.

Ayaha handed her bicycle to Shinobu, quickly explaining, "I crashed into him on the way back from my lesson. The tire wouldn't move, my cell phone fell into a puddle and broke—and I skinned my knee. Could you check Kenta, Shino? I think he hurt his leg."

"Sure thing. You'd better take a bath, Aya. You're covered in mud, and you'll catch cold like that," Shinobu warned, handing Ayaha the umbrella.

Ayaha took the umbrella and hurried inside, suddenly embarrassed by her own appearance.

Over the sound of her footsteps crunching on gravel, Ayaha heard Shinobu say, "Come in, Usui."

15

However, Kenta didn't recognize Shinobu and hesitated. "Um . . ."

"Shinobu Kirioka—from class B. I see you at the library sometimes. We can loan you a towel, an umbrella, and a change of clothes. My clothes might be a little small for you, but I imagine you can squeeze into some sweatpants. You should get that leg looked at."

"Yeah, but—"

"Seriously, we don't mind."

Ayaha didn't hear anything else. Kenta must've gone inside. She knew Shinobu would take care of him. She headed for the bathroom, where she scowled at herself in the mirror. "I look terrible!" Her usually fluffy waves of caramel brown hair were now wet and clinging to her—and there was a streak of mud on one cheek. She was furious with herself for letting Kenta see her like this. She at least should have wiped her face with a handkerchief. As she continued examining herself in the mirror, she couldn't help but notice her big eyes that radiated with light, her pale skin that matched her brightly colored hair, and her gently curved lips that resembled a Cupid's arrow. Kenta couldn't have objected to those attributes.

Lathering a dollop of facial foam, Ayaha glanced at the clock on the wall. If she took a fast shower and went out without drying her hair, she might get to see Kenta again before he left. Ayaha knew perfectly well that she would never do that, though. She couldn't bear to let him see her again unless everything were perfect.

Shinobu had said that he would loan Kenta an umbrella and a change of clothes, which meant Kenta would have to return them eventually. And Ayaha and Kenta might see each other at school. She could show him how great she could look then.

"I am beautiful, aren't I?" she asked the mirror. Of course, it didn't say anything, but the image it reflected back was answer enough to satisfy Ayaha.

 **MEET CHIBI VAMPIRE'S RIVAL**

A week after the end of summer vacation, the bombardment of cicada song showed no sign of abating. The summer had been particularly hot, and the Shiihaba First High uniform—a jumperskirt worn over a blouse—was horribly uncomfortable.

"Ugh! No matter how early I leave the house, I'm covered in sweat by the time I get to school." Karin Maaka shielded her eyes with one hand, glaring in the general direction of the baleful sun. The reason she had left the house fifteen minutes early wasn't to avoid the sun, however—she was trying to avoid bumping into Kenta Usui, who lived near her house. *If I run into him, what should I do?*

In August, Karin had thrown herself on Kenta. Obviously, it wasn't because her romantic passion had gotten the better of her. It was because her vampire instincts had gone out of control. Karin appeared to be an ordinary high school girl, but she wasn't actually human. She was the eldest daughter of a family of vampires that had migrated to Japan from the continent two hundred years prior. Her younger sister was still underage, and her own vampiric instincts hadn't yet awoken, but Karin's father, mother, and older brother all were full-fledged vampires who ruled the night and avoided the sun.

Karin wasn't like her family, though. Although she was a vampire, she had no problems with sunlight or garlic, had no control over bats, and couldn't erase human memories. The biggest difference between Karin and other vampires was that she didn't drink human blood. Not only that—for some reason, the amount of blood in her body was constantly increasing. If she didn't do anything about it, her blood pressure would increase so much that the blood vessels in her nose would rupture, causing blood to spray out of her nose before she collapsed. To avoid regular bouts of bloody-nose-induced anemia, Karin would bite people and inject her excess blood into them. She was a reverse vampire.

Last month, when her instincts were raging out of control, she'd pushed Kenta over—even though she didn't want to attack him at all. *It was so close. Just thinking about it makes me sweat!* Every time she remembered what had happened, she went flush, and sweat would pour down her forehead and the back of her neck. This time was no different. As Karin hurriedly dabbed her face with her handkerchief, she heard a voice.

"What has you flustered this early, Karin?"

"Aiiieeee!" Panic-stricken after realizing that the voice behind her was Kenta's, Karin waved around both arms wildly.

"Yikes! Ow!"

Kenta staggered backward, groaning.

Seeing Kenta in pain made Karin feel even more flustered. She'd been waving her hands around while one of them was still clutching her school bag. "S-sorry! Did I hit you?"

"You really have to stop waving your arms around like that. You didn't hit me this time, but still."

"But you said, 'Ow!'"

"I twisted my ankle yesterday. When I put my weight on it, it hurt, but that's not your fault."

"Are you okay? Should I carry your bag?" Karin had been embarrassed at the idea of speaking to him before, but when she heard he was injured, her concern won out. She held out her hand, but Kenta shook his head.

"It's not that serious. I got it taped up, and it'll be fine in a couple days. Don't worry."

The strange thing was that Kenta looked awfully pale for that to be true. That wasn't the only odd thing—the chance of rain had been less than ten percent, but he had a long umbrella with him. And judging from the logo on the handle and the shine of the fabric, the umbrella was a rather expensive brand. Kenta was barely able to make ends meet, much less afford something like that.

"Where'd you get the umbrella?" Karin asked, puzzled.

Kenta's face clouded over. "Do you know Shinobu Kirioka in class B?"

"No . . ."

"I guess you don't know many boys. I'd seen him around, but hadn't known his name. He loaned me this yesterday. Not only the umbrella—my clothes were soaked, so he loaned me a spare set, and taped up my sprained ankle for me."

"How nice of him! Good."

"Not so good. Kirioka is fine, but his cousin . . . I might have to pay for her bicycle."

In response to Karin's surprise, Kenta explained how he'd hurt his ankle running out in front of her bicycle, and how her bike had stopped working. "She's a second year girl named Ayaha Ougimachi. She yelled at me for bolting out of a side street, so I carried the bike to her house. She was in a hurry to take a shower and wanted to avoid catching cold, so we didn't discuss it yesterday—but I have to go by her room today and apologize."

"So, that's why you left the house so early?" Karin's own plot to leave early in order to avoid Kenta had backfired.

"I hope she'll let me off with an apology, but she seemed pretty incensed. I don't have much hope. How much does a new bicycle cost, anyway?"

If Ayaha had wanted a good bicycle, it could cost a lot more than the standard ten thousand or twenty thousand yen. Karin wished she could help Kenta, but when it came to money, it was out of the question. She wasn't as poor as he was, but her parents were vampires and didn't work—they had no source of income. Karin didn't receive an allowance. She had to work part time to pay for her own things—and for the electric bill. She was the only one without night vision and the only one in her house who ever turned on the lights. "Oh dear . . ." Karin sighed, worried.

The distress in Karin's eyes reminded Kenta of an earlier thought. "Oh yeah! Karin, a minute ago you had a very strange expression on your face. Is something wrong?"

"Eh . . . n-no . . ." Karin muttered, frantically shaking her head. She couldn't admit that she'd been worrying about *him*.

"Okay," Kenta replied, deciding to drop the subject. He proceeded to walk on, mumbling things like "installments?" and "temp job" to himself, wondering how he could possibly pay for the bike.

Karin glanced up at him. *Is there anything I can do for him?* She wanted to help.

Kenta Usui knew what Karin was. Anyone else would have been terrified to learn someone close to him was a vampire, and would have tried to drive the undead out of town—but not Kenta. He'd comforted

Karin when she'd started to cry, promised to keep her true identity secret, and also agreed to help look after her during the day, when the other Maaka vampires were unable to move.

To thank Kenta for keeping her secret, Karin had been bringing him lunch, but she didn't think that was nearly enough. *And when he tried to help me this summer, I pushed him down and almost bit him. Argh! So embarrassing!*

At the time, Karin's blood rush had reached the breaking point, and she had to bite and inject someone—but she'd waited too long. Her brain had been drowning in a sea of blood, and she couldn't think straight. Kenta had been passing by, noticed her condition, and pulled her into a deserted area so no one would see her nosebleed. But Karin's instincts had overwhelmed her, and she'd thrown herself on top of him. The only reason she'd been able to stop herself from biting him was the sense of shame that had somehow overtaken her mind despite her complete loss of reason.

In order to inject someone, Karin had to wrap her arms around the person and sink her teeth into the victim's throat. Similar to riding a crowded train and being uncomfortably close, it was doable if she were with a complete stranger, but it was too awkward and uncomfortable with someone she knew. She couldn't do it. And Karin didn't think of Kenta as merely a friend. His hesitant, delicate kindness had captured her heart over time. *If I bit him, I'd be too embarrassed to ever speak to him again. . . .*

It was awkward enough when the fall term started and Kenta had demanded an explanation. She couldn't run away, so she'd managed to tell him how she'd been so close to her limit that she'd lost all reason, to which Kenta replied, "If you need to bite someone, feel free to bite me." Taken aback, Karin thought, *I can't do that! I can't put my arms around him and bite him. Wouldn't that bother him?*

Apparently, Kenta didn't think of Karin as any different than a stranger on a train. Or was he actually embarrassed, but hiding it to make her like him? *I'm so stupid. I know that isn't possible,* she thought. *First of all, I can never go out with a boy. I'm not human!*

Not long after the start of the fall term, the other girls found out that Karin had been bringing Kenta lunch, and they'd demanded to know whether they were a couple. They'd all been in favor of the idea, but Karin had denied having any feelings for Kenta. Whether the girls had believed her was another story. *But I'm a vampire! Falling in love with Kenta is like . . . like a gorilla in love with an orangutan—completely impossible!* she'd thought.

Regardless of what her feelings were, if Kenta was in trouble, Karin wanted to help. He was always helping her, so she wanted to give something back.

Maybe I could work more hours. But if I offered him money, would he take it? Maybe it would end up hurting his pride. Argh, this is so tricky. Anyway . . . did he say "Ougimachi"? Maybe if I went with him to apologize . . .

Karin's and Kenta's legs carried them down the familiar route in silence. They'd nearly reached the school and were so early that there were hardly any students on the street outside the front gates. A mid-sized sedan glided past them, stopping in front of the gate. The passenger door opened, and a boy in Shiihaba First High's summer uniform quickly climbed out and opened the back door.

When Kenta saw the thin boy, he stopped. "Kirioka."

"Hmm? The one you mentioned? Then . . ." Karin knew the girl that climbed out of the car second must have been Shinobu Kirioka's cousin, Ayaha Ougimachi—the girl Kenta had crashed into. Karin stared at her. *She's so pretty!*

Karin was barely five feet tall, and this girl looked at least a hand higher. Waves of shiny brown hair were held elegantly in place with a barrette that perfectly matched her gorgeous features. As Ayaha climbed out of the car and bent down to speak through the car window, every motion was graceful and a pleasure to behold.

"Auntie, thank you for driving us," Ayaha said graciously.

"Don't worry about it! You're injured, Aya! Shino, you take care of her. You're a good boy, so I hardly have to tell you." It was easy for Karin to hear what was going on because the middle-aged woman in the driver's seat had a voice that carried well.

"Yes, yes," Shinobu replied with an annoyed grimace as he took his cousin's bag. Ayaha acted as though having her bags toted for her was perfectly natural.

As the car drove away, Kenta groaned. "She mentioned hurting her ankle. Is it so bad that she can't walk? If they want me to pay the doctor's bill, as well . . ." He was visibly deflating.

"B-but she's not on crutches. It's probably nothing!" Karin exclaimed, trying to cheer up Kenta. She absentmindedly tugged at his sleeve, failing to realize that her voice was more shrill than she'd intended.

Overhearing the pair's conversation, Ayaha turned toward them.

Kenta awkwardly muttered, "Sorry again about yesterday—"

"You have a lot of nerve!" Ayaha interrupted, frowning angrily. "First, you injure me, and then, you come to school all happy happy?"

"What? I'm not—"

"I guess I was wrong about you. Idiot! Womanizer!" she yelled before running inside the school.

Kenta's mouth was agape, and Karin was equally taken aback. "Womanizer" was the last word she ever would've used to describe Kenta.

They heard someone laughing and glanced over to find Shinobu doubled over, beside himself with laughter.

"What's so funny, Kirioka?" Kenta asked, wearing a fearsome scowl—but not even that was enough to stop Shinobu.

"Sorry, sorry . . . that was too much! Is that the umbrella from yesterday?"

"Oh, yeah. Thanks a lot, really. I'll bring the clothes tomorrow, after we wash them." Kenta was still angry about being laughed at, but he remembered how much help Shinobu had been the day before as he clumsily handed back the umbrella.

"Don't worry about it."

"Um . . . is Ougimachi badly injured? So much that she couldn't walk to school?"

"Hardly. You saw her run off a second ago, right? My mother loves her like a pet cat and overreacted. And Aya loves to be spoiled. Yesterday, she complained that her elbow and ankle hurt, but I looked them over, and they were only slightly banged up. Your ankle is much worse."

"Oh . . . well, I'm glad she wasn't hurt. How about the bicycle? I hope you'll let me pay for it in installments. Would you ask her about that for me?"

Kenta inquired, bowing his head. It was much easier to ask Shinobu, who was the same age and gender, than Ayaha, who was obviously furious.

Shinobu blinked at Kenta, puzzled. "Pay? What do you mean? Aya said she fell over on her own."

"Huh?"

"She said that her tires slipped on the wet road, she spun out of control, and her bike slammed into your leg. She insisted the injuries and damage to the bike weren't your fault."

"R-really? But she seemed so angry . . . I wonder why," Kenta mumbled.

Karin wondered the same thing. After all, Ayaha had clearly said, "First, you injure me" a moment earlier. It didn't sound anything like what Shinobu was saying.

Shinobu glanced from Kenta to Karin with a mischievous glimmer in his eye. "That's your fault for coming to school hand in hand with your adorable girlfriend."

"Wha—?" Kenta's face turned brick red.

Karin staggered backward—not because she'd been mistaken for Kenta's girlfriend, but because she had followed Shinobu's gaze and realized she was still holding on to Kenta's sleeve. Letting go instantly, her face felt as though it were on fire, and her brain seemed to be overheating, too. She was unable to think of anything to say in her defense. You'd think she'd just finished running a marathon the way her heart was beating.

Kenta recovered first. "Don't be stupid! We weren't holding hands!"

"Let's not have a shouting contest in front of the gate, Usui. I may have exaggerated a little, but you did come to school with her," Shinobu pointed out.

"We live near each other. I accidentally bumped into her on the way through the nature preserve! She's not my girlfriend!"

"Ohhh?" Shinobu replied, overemphasizing his doubt.

Karin shook her head so violently that her flapping hair made an audible noise. "R-r-really! Kenta and I aren't like that!"

"Aw, okay. Sorry for the dumb joke, Maaka," Shinobu said.

"It wasn't only dumb, Kirioka—it was kind of rude. What if somebody had believed you?" Kenta wailed, glowering at Shinobu's irrepressible smirk.

Karin didn't find Kenta's negative reaction any less troubling than the accusation itself. *You don't need to deny it so emphatically!* It was true that she wasn't Kenta's girlfriend, but when he'd corrected Shinobu's mistake, Kenta at least could have hesitated or blushed—or given some sort of indication that he secretly wished she were his girlfriend. *Wh-what am I thinking? Am I wishing Kenta . . . no, no, no, no!* Karin pressed her hands against her flushed cheeks. She'd indulged herself merely by imagining the scenario, and she felt very embarrassed. Her heart was beating uncomfortably fast.

Being different species wasn't the only thing preventing their relationship—Karin was unable to get close to Kenta. In the same way that vampires feel their appetites awaken when they're around a particular type of blood, Karin's blood began to increase rapidly when she was around anyone who was unhappy. And for some reason, a cloud of unhappiness had always enveloped Kenta. Karin tried to avoid close contact with him, and had warned him that he set off her blood rush so that he would keep his distance, but she'd been distracted by his worried expression and forgot. *Ack! I've been too close to him all this time! Is that why the rhythm of my heartbeat has been so violent?* Karin hurriedly stepped away. The boys were still talking about the bicycle, and neither one noticed that she'd moved.

"I don't think we need you to pay for anything. My mother loves buying things for Aya—and Aya's dad probably would buy her a car if she asked for it," explained Shinobu.

"She lives with you and not her parents? I mean, not to pry or anything . . ." Kenta asked, suddenly realizing that his question might not be appropriate.

Shinobu chuckled. "It's no great secret. She got pissed off at her dad and wound up living with us. She's spent loads of time here ever since she was a child. My mother always wanted a girl, but she only managed to have me—so she dotes on her niece. And Aya is very comfortable with adoration. I'd better swing her bag by her class before the bell rings. See you later." Holding both bags, Shinobu walked off in the direction of the second year classrooms.

Karin and Kenta exchanged glances.

"Good, you don't have to pay," sighed Karin.

"Yeah, what a relief. I'd still better go apologize at lunch, though. It was my fault for running out in front of her, after all. If I hadn't done that, Ougimachi never would have fallen off her bike. If she were going to lie and claim it was all her fault, why would she get so angry? I don't get it." Kenta shook his head.

Karin didn't understand it, either. She didn't think Kenta had said anything that would put Ayaha in a bad mood. She'd been angry before he'd opened his mouth, and she'd run off after yelling at him. Shinobu seemed to know, but . . . *Wait, what had he said? "That's your fault for coming to school hand in hand with your girlfriend." What? Wait—that means . . . Ougimachi is . . .* Karin reeled as though she'd been tasered. Thinking back, Ayaha's furious expression had been directed more toward her than Kenta. *She thought I was Kenta's girlfriend? And that's why she got so angry and called him a womanizer? Then she's . . . in l-l-love with . . . with Kenta?*

It was a possibility. No—it was the only explanation. Karin's heart rate had started to slow now that she wasn't standing next to Kenta, but it began to accelerate again. Kenta said that he'd carried the broken bike back to Ayaha's house after the accident. He might look a little frightening, but inside he was very good-natured, with a strong sense of responsibility—Karin knew this better than anyone. If Ayaha had noticed Kenta's true nature on the way home, it was only natural that she would've fallen for him. *I wonder what Kenta thinks of her . . . ?*

She might've been angry, but Ayaha Ougimachi was beautiful—and unlike Karin, she was human. There was nothing to stop him from loving her. And Kenta might feel obligated to Ayaha for taking the blame for the accident. The misunderstanding about Karin's relationship with Kenta would be cleared up quickly once she spoke to Shinobu—in which case, Kenta and Ayaha could start going out at any time.

Once he had a girlfriend, Kenta wouldn't have time to clean up Karin's messes the way he had been. The thoughts weighed on the reverse vampire's chest like an iron plate. *Kenta . . .* She'd never expected her love to bear fruit, but was she going to lose him as a friend, too?

"Karin, we should be getting to class," Kenta hollered.

Forcing a smile, Karin replied, "Go ahead. I was too close to you earlier."

"Ah! Your blood rush? Sorry, I didn't think . . . I'll keep my distance today."

Kenta strode away into the school, and Karin watched him go, sighing feebly. She had never told Kenta what emotion set off her instincts. She considered it extremely cruel to point out to someone how unhappy he was. Karin didn't know exactly what it was that made him so unhappy, though.

When they'd first met, Karin had tried to figure out how to make Kenta happy, hoping that doing so would bring peace to her life again. But once she'd started to fall in love with him, she'd stopped thinking about it. *This is good . . . if Kenta gets a girlfriend, that might make him happy, and he won't set off my blood rush anymore. I can be like I was before he transferred here.* It wasn't a big deal—Karin repeated that to herself over and over.

Meanwhile, outside class 2-C, Ayaha was leaning against the wall, biting her lip and glaring at her fingernails, glancing occasionally at the stairs. Anyone who saw her would assume she was sulking—she knew that perfectly well. She was maintaining her pose for Shinobu, who would arrive any minute.

After six minutes and forty-two seconds, Shinobu finally came up the stairs. Ayaha turned to yell at him for taking so long.

Shinobu shoved the bag toward her. "You forgot this." He didn't attempt to comfort her at all.

Ayaha knew her cousin was never upset or flustered about anything, but in that moment, his lack of sympathy was incredibly annoying. In retaliation, she directed all the gloom inside herself toward him. "What was that? He didn't tell me about *her!*"

Shinobu smirked. "Nobody brags about their girlfriends without being asked."

"But—!"

"Yes, yes—calm down. There are too many people here. Let's talk over there," Shinobu suggested, guiding her away from the stares of the students walking down the hallway. He didn't speak again until they were in the breezeway. "The girl with Usui was Karin Maaka. She's in the same class as Usui. She didn't make many waves at first, but since the end of first term, the guys have started to notice her. She's getting pretty popular."

"Why?"

"Because her tits doubled in size. Lots of guys like petite girls with big boobs. Not that it's easy to tell how big they are with these uniforms, but

I'd guess she's easily an F cup—assuming she isn't wearing a push-up bra."

Ayaha glanced down at her own chest. Her slender frame with long legs and arms was the ideal body type for a ballerina. She had nothing against her teacup-sized breasts—they matched her figure well. But compared to the first year girl's bountiful bosom, it was hard to view a B cup as anything but inadequate.

Without considering what Ayaha might be thinking, Shinobu leaned against the railing of the walkway, gazing down into the garden, and continued: "Apparently, Maaka is making lunches for Usui. She insists that she's making them to thank Usui for helping her, but all the girls in D class are certain she's in love with him."

"Oh no!" Ayaha's mind went blank. "How could you, Shino? If you knew all that, why didn't you say so yesterday?"

"I didn't need to. Usui insisted Maaka wasn't his girlfriend."

"Wha—" The direction of Ayaha's anger had been knocked off course completely, and she could only gape at her cousin.

"He said that they live near each other. They bumped into each other on their way through the nature preserve, and coincidentally reached the school at the same time. No matter how people think Maaka feels, it doesn't mean anything unless Usui feels the same. As far as I can tell, Usui doesn't think of Maaka as anything but a friend at the moment."

Ayaha's raging emotions became placid. Shinobu gazed up at her through his glasses with a smile in his eyes. "You're a beautiful girl, Aya. Strangers hit on you all the time—and you've been approached by talent scouts who you've turned down. You're a lot better looking than most girls. You think so, too, don't you?"

"Well, yeah," she nodded, running her fingers through her hair, embarrassed. "I mean, don't get the wrong idea, Shino—it's not as if I'm in love with Usui. But I didn't like seeing him getting all mushy with some girl. That's all."

"I know. Oh, I told Usui that he didn't need to pay for the bike. You don't mind, do you?"

"No. Auntie said she'd buy a new one."

"You aren't going to ask your father? It might be a good excuse to patch up things between you—"

"Shut up, Shino! I'm not calling him until he apologizes!" Ayaha shouted. She wanted to forget about the situation with her father. "As long as that crass woman is pretending she can replace my mother, I'm not going home!"

"Yeah, yeah—okay. I shouldn't have said anything. The point is that Usui doesn't have to pay for the bike. He was really happy. I'd heard he was working a lot of part-time jobs, but I guess he really is hard up."

"Really?"

"Yeah. I've never seen anyone else wearing patched socks before."

Ayaha thoughtfully put her index finger to her chin. Between Kenta Usui's frightening exterior veiling his sweet nature and his financial troubles, it really did sound as though he were cursed. *In* The Nutcracker *and* Swan Lake, *the curse is defeated by love—but it's not like I'm in love with Usui, of course. Patched socks? How sad . . .*

There was nothing strange about being nice to unfortunate people. Ayaha decided that she would go to Kenta's room at lunch and tell him herself that he didn't have to pay for the bike and that her injuries were no big deal—so he didn't need to worry. She was sure he would be relieved.

The warning bell rang from the speaker above Ayaha and Shino.

"Okay, Aya. I have to get to class—homeroom's starting," Shino announced.

Finally taking her bag from Shino, Ayaha began to walk away, but turned back. "Shino, which class is Usui?"

"He's in D—but if you're going to see him at lunch, you'd better be fast. D class has PE fifth period, and they'll be out of there pretty quickly. It might be easier during a regular break."

Ayaha's cousin thought of everything—he always had. He drove off the bullies, helped her with homework, and gave her perfect advice when she was having trouble with her ballet technique. The other day, her period had started suddenly while they were out and had stained her skirt. She'd started crying, but he'd taken her to the bathroom in a nearby shopping center and returned ten minutes later with pads and a change of clothes. If Ayaha asked Shinobu, he would take care of anything—she firmly believed that. *If we were in the same grade, he could help me even more. He was born three months after me—that's the only problem with him.* This time, it had worked in her favor. Shino had been able to tell her all about Kenta Usui. If he'd been in the same grade, he'd never have known about the girl hanging around him.

"Thanks, Shino. Bye." Ayaha dashed off to class, satisfied.

Watching her go, Shinobu muttered with a trace of rueful hopelessness in his voice, "Kenta Usui, huh? He's a different type than the others . . . but how soon will she get bored this time?"

Karin had no way of knowing that Ayaha and Shinobu were talking about her, but questions about Kenta also swirled around her mind. *Does Ayaha like Kenta? I'm sure she does. Kenta's so nice. It only stands to reason that girls would fall in love with him.*

Sitting in class, Karin couldn't think of anything else. She didn't want to think about it, but her thoughts were trapped in a loop. Ayaha's elegant features, graceful movements, and slender figure flashed through Karin's mind again and again. *What does Kenta think of her? I guess there's no point in speculating. . . .* Karin remembered nothing about class. She was so out of it that she didn't even notice when the teacher called her name during third period English, and she was ordered to write a special report by the next day.

"What's wrong, Karin? Are you feeling okay?" her best friend Maki Tokitou whispered the moment the bell had rung and the teacher had left the classroom. She sat down in the seat in front of Karin, peering into her face. "You get anemic all the time, so try to take it easy. Maybe you should go to the nurse's office?"

"N-no, I'm fine. It's nothing—I'm just a little sleepy. And I can't miss science, because I don't want to take makeup exams two terms in a row."

"But . . . ah, okay. If you fall over in class, we'll make Usui take you to the nurse's office."

"Wh-why him?" Karin asked, flailing her arms around.

Suddenly, a sight as splendid as a peacock caught Karin's attention. Surprised, she leaned toward the door. Ayaha Ougimachi had walked in. She was wearing the same white blouse and black jumper skirt as everyone else, but she stood out. There was certainly something about her that caught the eye. Karin wasn't the only one who thought so. Most of the students— particularly the boys—had stopped talking to turn and stare. *Wh-why is she in a first year classroom?*

Without so much as glancing at Karin, Ayaha glanced around the room, walking directly to Kenta's seat in the back row. Kenta had a textbook open on the desk in front of him, and he only glanced up when he noticed Ayaha standing in front of him.

Kenta quickly jumped to his feet, bowing his head. "Sorry about yesterday. Kirioka said that I don't have to pay for the bike, but . . ."

"Yes, my aunt will buy me a new one, so you don't need to worry about that. And I'm not badly hurt, so I forgive you for the accident. You can relax."

If Ayaha hadn't been so beautiful, her haughty tone surely would have prompted someone to ask if she believed herself to be queen.

As pleased as Kenta was to hear that Ayaha no longer held him responsible for the accident, he wasn't quite sure how to respond to her commanding manner. "Uh, um . . . thank you," he stammered.

Apparently, Ayaha had expected more of a response. She frowned slightly, but recovered a moment later, and added, "To thank you for carrying my bicycle, I'll join you for lunch. When fourth period ends, come to the cafeteria. I brought a lunch for myself, but I'll buy you any meal you want."

Listening from the side, Karin felt her heart tighten. On the way to school that morning, she'd given Kenta a lunch for the day. She could no longer pretend to ignore them. Glancing cautiously over her shoulder, Karin noticed that Kenta was scratching his head and appeared trapped.

"Um, thanks, but I already have a lunch," Kenta replied.

When Karin heard that, she felt a surge of joy that seemed to propel her body right into space. *Kenta would rather eat my lunch than have Ougimachi buy him lunch from the school cafeteria!* She felt her face softening, completely unaware that Maki had been watching her face and Kenta and Ayaha's interaction closely.

Once Ayaha had proposed something, though, she didn't give up on it easily. "Give it to someone else—or keep it for dinner."

"No, um, I . . . I don't . . . I didn't really do anything worthy of all this. S-sorry. I have to go to the bathroom." Kenta bowed his head to Ayaha and fled through the back doors.

One of the other boys in class shook his head. "What a waste," he muttered.

Ayaha couldn't exactly chase after Kenta if he were going to the bathroom. Scowling as she watched him leave, she turned around and left through the front doors.

Karin sighed.

Instantly, Maki stood up, biting her lip, and ran after Ayaha.

"Maki?" Karin exclaimed, sensing that something was up. She ran after Maki, but by the time she'd reached the hallway, Maki had caught up with Ayaha.

"Excuse me! About Usui . . ." Maki called out.

Ayaha stopped and turned around.

Maki got right to the point: "Just now, you said that your offer to buy Usui lunch was only to thank him. Are you really in love with him?"

"Who are you?" Ayaha asked.

"Maki Tokitou—same class as Usui. Someone else is already making lunches for Usui, so . . ."

Ayaha brushed back her hair, irritated. "So what! I know there's a girl making lunches for him, but I don't see why that should stop me from buying him lunch. And it certainly doesn't have anything to do with you."

"It certainly does. My best friend is the one making him lunch! She's very serious, so don't you go trying to steal him from her!"

"Uuugh! Maki, stop it!" Karin wailed, pouncing on her friend and covering her mouth with one hand. Maki's voice had been getting steadily louder. "But Karin, you—!"

"Forget it! Please!"

After watching the duo struggle for a few moments, Ayaha turned her gaze toward Karin. "So, you're the one? You were with Usui this morning, too. Maaka, was it?"

Ayaha was even more beautiful when viewed up close. Her elegance was overwhelming, and Karin felt her heart beat faster. Worried that her heartbeat was audible to those around her, Karin stammered a reply: "Y-yes . . ."

Clearly disapproving of Karin's timidity, Ayaha said scornfully, "My cousin Shino told me that Usui said you weren't his girlfriend—and that you only came to school together because you lived near each other. Is that true? Or was Usui lying, and you're actually going out?"

"He wasn't!" Karin blurted out forcefully. She couldn't bear for Kenta to be called a liar. The very thought of it made her sweat. "Kenta never lies."

"Oh. Then you *are* only a friend. You don't care what I do. I think you should tell your friend here to mind her own business."

"Wh—? You have—!" Maki started, but Karin gave her a fearsome glare.

Ayaha's face went flush as she stammered awkwardly: "B-but don't get the wrong idea. I don't have any . . . feelings for Usui. I ran into him on my bike yesterday, and he twisted his ankle . . . and one thing led to another, so he sort of . . . stuck with me . . ."

Karin's nemesis had partially turned away from her and Maki, but Ayaha's face in profile made Karin's heart thump louder than before. *Huh? Wait, is this . . . ?*

At that moment, the bell signaling the end of break rang. Ayaha turned without another word, squared up her shoulders, and walked down the hall.

Maki glanced up gloomily. "Argh! Just because she's a year older doesn't give her the right to act so arrogant!"

"Forget it, Maki. We have to get back to class. The teacher's coming," Karin replied, tugging her friend's sleeve.

Maki gave a gloomy glance. "Sorry, Karin. I got carried away again. I shouldn't have done that."

Karin already knew the reason behind Maki's outburst. A few days before, Maki had seen Karin handing Kenta a lunch, and had been really happy that her old friend had finally started dating a boy. Karin had been too shy to talk to boys, and Maki had been forced to cover for her, so this was understandable. But in her joy, Maki had told the other girls in class, and they all had come running to Karin, demanding to know if it was true. Cornered, Karin had blabbed, "I don't like him!" but Kenta had overheard, and the shock of that made Karin burst into tears. As a result, Maki felt that she had gone overboard. She'd apologized, but Karin knew that Maki hadn't meant to cause any problems, and she'd forgiven her at once.

It seemed that deep in Maki's heart was a protective desire to make Karin's first love a success. "That girl was so full of herself—the worst kind of pretty girl! Usui was so indecisive, and you were so panic-stricken that I had to say something. Sorry."

"N-no—don't say that. Kenta and I really are only friends." Karin was glad that she had Maki's support, but she and Kenta were different species and could never be more than friends. More than with Maki's behavior, Karin's mind was preoccupied with Ayaha, who'd left in a huff. *She isn't happy. . . .* They'd been close enough for Karin to tell. Ayaha had some sort of unhappiness hanging over her—enough to make Karin's blood increase and her heart beat faster. *Um . . . when was the last time I ejected any . . . ?*

That morning, Karin had used her blood rush as an excuse to avoid Kenta, but now that she thought about it, the last time she'd bitten someone was near the end of August. Previously, she'd only needed to eject blood once a month, but after she'd learned that unhappy people triggered the blood rush, her sensitivity to it had increased, and the time lag had decreased. *I still should have a few days, but I think I'd better not take any chances. If my blood increases too much and my mind goes blank again today . . . oh no—I'm working late today. And I have to leave directly from the final homeroom to make my shift on time.*

Karin didn't want to try to find a target after work. She was too scared to wander around at night trying to find someone alone. She might get mixed up in something weird, but it was mostly the darkness that bothered her. Karin knew it was unusual for a vampire to be scared of the dark, but that didn't stop it from being true. *Hmm . . . well, I haven't reached my limit yet, so I'll have to bite someone tomorrow—or the day after. Today, I'll go home and ask Anju to help.*

Drifting back into the classroom, Karin tried to balance her condition with her schedule. *I have to avoid unhappy people until I can bite someone!* She definitely would have to keep her distance from Kenta—a thought that caused a tiny pain in her chest.

As hot as it was, it wasn't quite mid-summer, and the sun's rays had lost a lot of their strength. Partly because of the gentle breeze, it was cool enough in the shade on the concrete roof at midday.

"Oh! Chicken cutlets and dry curry?" Kenta exclaimed to himself, opening his lunch. There were raisins scattered on the dry curry, with bite-size chicken cutlets on the side. There also was a tiny salad, with broccoli and cherry tomatoes, and because Karin worried that Kenta might tire of all the Western-style food, she'd packed a tiny tinfoil cup filled with pickled burdock.

The day before, there had been several varieties of sandwiches, including seafood and potato salad; and the day before that, there was a traditional Japanese cooked salted salmon with soy sauce, boiled vegetables, and rolled eggs.

"Itadakimasu!" Thanking the gods for sending Karin his way, Kenta quickly popped a piece of chicken into his mouth. The crispy coating melted on his tongue, and the juicy meat inside sent waves of pleasure through his mind and stomach. He had skipped breakfast, and his stomach had been screaming for food. Kenta chewed the chicken several times before swallowing, and was about to place the next piece into his mouth when he heard a voice.

"Now, now—a lunch that looks that delicious ought to be savored," declared the voice.

Kenta almost did a spit take. Slapping one hand across his mouth, he barely managed to keep the food in.

It was Shinobu Kirioka, who apparently had mastered the art of opening doors soundlessly. He calmly sat down next to Kenta and opened his own lunch.

"Wh-what are you doing here?" Kenta asked, finally swallowing his chicken.

"Do I look like I'm here to play gateball? I'm opening my lunch. One can assume I plan to eat it," Shinobu replied. He glanced at Kenta's lunch and smirked. "Someone worked hard on that. Nutrition, flavor, *and* appearance? If she's only doing that out of gratitude, Maaka must be a real philanthropist—or an incredibly devoted cook."

Kenta's chopsticks froze. He was glad it was only broccoli he'd picked up. If it had been a cherry tomato, he undoubtedly would have dropped it. "How do you know Karin made it?"

"Tokitou and Naito from your class saw her hand it to you, and they told Yamamoto, who told Ootani and Kida—and they told the other people in class, who told the girls in B class, who told me."

Such a matter-of-fact reply silenced Kenta. He didn't know what to make of Shinobu Kirioka. There was something about him that Kenta simply didn't like. The gleam in Shinobu's eyes behind his thin rectangular glasses seemed to drag everything one was hiding out into the light of day.

The day before, Shinobu had loaned Kenta an umbrella and a change of clothes, and had taped up his ankle. It seemed generous enough on the surface, but was Kenta right to feel slightly unsettled by it? It seemed like a good idea to eat quickly and leave the roof.

Kenta tried to turn his attention back to his food, but Shinobu interrupted him: "According to the girls, Maaka is in love with you and is using the lunches to win your heart."

Practically choking on dry curry, Kenta grabbed his old water bottle that he'd been refilling from the tap and poured water down his throat to try to dislodge the food. Between coughing fits, he stammered, "D-don't say weird things when someone is about to swallow! It'd be a waste to spit out this food!"

"Sorry. It wasn't intentional, I swear. Pure coincidence."

Liar. Kenta took another sip of water, glaring at Shinobu bitterly. *Karin, in love with me? How can that be? Tokitou told me that Karin had no experience with boys. Someone like that wouldn't turn around and fall in love so easily.*

It was true that Karin could talk to Kenta, although she barely managed to stammer when she spoke to other boys—but that was probably because he knew what she was. Because she didn't have to hide anything from Kenta, she could relax. That was all it was.

Shinobu let his gaze wander thoughtfully toward the sky, nodding. "Yeah, I thought it was probably a rumor."

"O-oh. Well . . . fine."

"If Maaka were in love with you, you'd never take the lunches from her. If you had the kind of personality that could leech off a daily offering like that, you'd never have turned down Aya's offer to buy you lunch."

"How do you know about that?"

"Aya texted me during fourth period, yelling at me because you ran away."

"What do you mean?"

"She said that I have to go eat cake with her this afternoon, before her ballet lesson. Aya can eat anything she wants without gaining weight, so she always stuffs herself when she's angry. She said she was going to see you again at lunch, but since you're eating up here, you must have dodged her. She'll be even more pissed."

Kenta was stunned.

"You should've eaten with her once. Aya's pretty and she gets a decent allowance. I don't think it would do you any harm to be in her company."

"If you like her so much, *you* go out with her," Kenta snapped. He felt as though Shinobu were making fun of his poverty, rubbing Ayaha's allowance in his face.

"I'm kidding. Aya's my cousin. She blurts stuff out, gets all puffed up, and never thinks things through. If she were to go out with someone I know . . . the very thought gives me chills."

"Not much of a recommendation," Kenta said. "Forget going out with her. I can't let someone buy me lunch without good reason."

"It's not like she'd be buying you a full-course dinner at a five-star restaurant. It's the school cafeteria— nothing to get stubborn about."

"I'm not talking about the amount of money. I'm not a sponge."

"But you're getting lunches from Maaka. Is there a good reason for that?"

If Kenta were to say something careless, Shinobu would twist around whatever he said and make the conversation more difficult to get through. Kenta silently munched away on his chicken cutlets and took a drink of water.

Seemingly unworried about Kenta's lack of response, Shinobu continued: "She's not your girlfriend. Maaka said that she was making you lunches to pay you back for something. But what could you have done for her that would deserve a lunch every day? Did you cover up a crime for her?"

This time, Kenta did spit out his food, coughing violently.

"Want me to pat your back?"

"*Hack* . . . ugh . . . damn you . . . *hack* . . ."

"I guess I deserve that. Okay, I'll drop it. And you don't need to yell at me like you did this morning for spreading negative rumors about Maaka. It was merely an example—a pretty bad one, I admit. We'll leave it at some sort of secret."

The one good thing about Kenta's coughing fit was that it freed him from having to respond. The fact that his hand was covering his mouth, hiding his expression, wasn't bad, either. However, Shinobu wasn't one to overlook the subtlest of reactions.

"Hmm . . . so there's a secret? And the depth of planning in the lunches—payment for your silence?"

There was a danger buzzer going off in Kenta's ears, timed to match his coughing. *Does he suspect something?* He tried to sneak a peak at Shinobu's expression. Shinobu appeared to have a keenly interested smile, but what exactly he found interesting was impossible to discern. *He doesn't believe the rumors that Karin and I are going out. But in that case . . . he knows there must be a good reason for her to make me lunch every day.*

If Kenta didn't figure out some way to distract him, Shinobu might work out what Karin was. Kenta wiped his mouth with the back of his hand. "No secrets and no payments for silence. I told you how Karin and I live near each other, right? And we're in the same class—and we work at the same job."

"Yeah, I know."

"Her mom and dad asked me to look after her. She's a bit of a klutz—she's always falling down and breaking things—and she gets sick a lot. If she gets hurt, or anemic, she needs someone to carry her to the sick room."

"I see."

"And she had all those makeup tests at the end of the first term. I helped her study. The lunches are thanks for all that." Kenta was hiding some things, but he was basically telling the truth—which meant he could speak calmly, without averting his gaze.

Shinobu shrugged. "So, as far as you're concerned, it's just a business relationship?"

"Will you stop using words like 'secret' and 'relationship'? You can dig all you want, but there's nothing there." Finished eating at last, Kenta snapped his lunchbox shut and stood up. The more he talked, the more likely he was to let something slip. "Bye."

"Say 'hi' to Maaka for me."

"What do you mean?" asked Kenta.

"You're in her class, right?"

Everything Shinobu said seemed to have a double meaning. There was no point in trying to figure him out. Kenta went through the door and down the stairs, thinking. *He used Karin's name deliberately . . .* Kenta had seen Shinobu in the library before, and had spoken to him two or three times before, but that was the extent of it. They were hardly close. But nonetheless, Shinobu had deliberately joined Kenta for lunch, asking a string of probing questions. *If he's interested in me, he doesn't need to ask about Karin. Or did Kirioka approach me to learn more about her?* That seemed to make more sense. *Maybe Karin did something dumb, and he learned what she really is. Maybe Kirioka saw her biting somebody and wondered if she might be a vampire, and then he came to me because I'm with her a lot. Hmm . . . it's possible.*

Kenta himself had seen Karin biting his mother and had grown suspicious. It wouldn't surprise him if someone else followed the same line of thought. *I'll have to warn her to watch out for Kirioka. I don't have any secrets that would interest him, really . . . I'm sure he's after her.*

Shinobu's strange choice of words probably had something to do with him suspecting what she was—Kenta was nearly sure of it now. He was tragically dense when it came to affairs of the heart, and never once connected Shinobu's words with Ayaha's puzzling attitude, but he couldn't come up with any other explanation.

Meanwhile, up on the roof, Shinobu glanced at the door Kenta had escaped through and smirked. "I can dig all I want? You're a fool, Usui. A line like that is only begging me to dig further. Now, which one has the secret? Usui—or Maaka?"

Clouds like thin, gray Japanese paper were plastered across the morning sky. It looked as though it could be raining by noon.

Karin glanced up at the small black shadow flitting through the trees. *Good thing it was cloudy today. If it had been sunny, Anju would still be asleep.*

Anju's vampiric powers hadn't yet been awakened, but it still hurt her to be in direct sunlight. She attended elementary school to learn about human society, but only when it was raining or cloudy. When the skies were clear, she spent the entire day asleep in bed. With the exception of herself, Karin's entire family was nocturnal.

Fortunately, today was cloudy, and her sister was attending school—which meant she was awake. She could send out her bats to help Karin. *I have to bite someone before I run into Kenta at school!* Karin had left the house thirty minutes early, hoping to find a target in the nature preserve. *It doesn't have to be someone unhappy—just someone by himself in a secluded area. Anyone at all . . . anyone besides Kenta.*

Karin remembered having talked to Kenta the day before at Julian. She'd known her blood would increase if she were near him, but given the topic of their discussion, they couldn't raise their voices. Specifically, it seemed as though Shinobu Kirioka might know what Karin was. *But I don't think I ever spoke to him before yesterday morning. Did I do anything suspicious—or did he happen to see me biting someone?* She had no idea what it could be, but she couldn't take any chances. She was very happy that Kenta was worried about her, but as a blood-injector, she couldn't afford to cling to Kenta out of sheer joy.

Karin and Kenta had only been whispering to each other for five minutes, but she had been close enough to his aura of unhappiness that her blood had begun to increase, causing her blood pressure and body temperature to rise. She also had begun to sweat and pant.

When Kenta had noticed, he coughed and tried to force himself to calm down, and then he'd told Karin that she should bite him. Biting someone who knew what she was made a lot of sense. Karin wouldn't need to erase Kenta's memories, and if she bit him somewhere secluded, there was no risk of being seen. But whatever the logic, she rejected the idea emotionally. She'd insisted she still had time and fled the scene. *How can I possibly put my arms around Kenta and bite him, knowing that he'd remember it afterward? No, no, no—that would be insanely embarrassing! Completely out of the question! It's much easier to bite someone I don't know!* The mere thought of it made Karin feverish. She shook her head violently, trying to drive the image out of her mind. She had to bite someone before she saw Kenta again, to get rid of her excess blood.

There still was one other thing bothering Karin. *What did Kenta think of Ougimachi coming to class at lunch yesterday?* At noon yesterday, Kenta had bolted out of the classroom, lunch in hand, the moment fourth period ended. Presumably, he'd remembered what Ayaha had suggested and was running to avoid meeting her. Karin had stayed in the classroom, eating with Maki and Fukumi, and sure enough—Ayaha came in. She had peered around the room, and then said something to a boy near the door. It was obvious that she'd asked where Kenta was. The boy shook his head, after which Ayaha appeared extremely irritated. Some brave boy had offered himself as Kenta's replacement, but he was flatly ignored.

The memory of this bothered Karin. *The feeling of unhappiness I got off her was so strong . . .* Karin's seat was nearly ten feet from the door, but she'd clearly felt her vampiric instincts whirring to life. *If Kenta not being there is enough to make Ougimachi unhappy, then she must really love him.*

Kenta hadn't returned until minutes before fifth period. The boys surrounded him, saying, "Dude, a hot girl wanted to buy you lunch!" and "What are you,

stupid?"—so he must have known she'd come. Perhaps
Karin should've asked Kenta about Ayaha while they'd
been whispering at Julian, but her blood rush had
forced her away from him, so she never got a chance
to mention it. No, even if her blood had been normal,
she never could've dared ask about Kenta's feelings. *If
Kenta had asked why I was asking about Ougimachi,
how could I answer? He doesn't think of me as anything
but a friend. Simply because I have these unrequited
feelings . . .*

Karin sighed, gazing around her immediate
vicinity. There was someone moving at her right. On
the grass to the side of the path was an aging man in
sweatpants, swinging a golf club. He was in the park,
so he wasn't using a ball—only practicing his swing.
She could hear him grunt with each swing as chunks
of dirt flew.

"Hmm . . . I'll never be able to play on a course like
this," the man muttered wistfully, stopping swinging to
wipe the sweat from his face with a towel. He must've
been practicing behind the bushes because he was just
starting, and was embarrassed that someone might see
his awkward swing.

Lucky! I'll bite him! Making sure Anju's bat was
still with her, Karin moved quietly forward onto the
grass. The man had his back to her and didn't see her
coming. *Okay!* The moment she dashed forward to
leap on him and bite down, the man swung his club

backward. The club head hit her on the shoulder, and she fell over backward. "Ugh!"

The man appeared even more surprised than Karin was. He cried out loudly, dropping his club and leaning forward to help her up. "Ahh! S-sorry! Are you okay?"

Oww! B-but now's my chance! Karin thought to herself as her target edged toward her. She wrapped her arms around the man, clinging to him.

"Wh-wh-wh-what are you doing?" It was obvious that this man was a very upright individual, and not the type to rejoice because a young girl had thrown her arms around him. He tried to push Karin away, but she couldn't let him escape and held on desperately. She had no choice after a most unexpected voice called out from the path behind her.

"Maaka? What are you *doing?*"

Karin jerked, twisting her head around. Staring at her wide-eyed was none other than Ayaha Ougimachi. *She saw me!* Once the strength had left Karin's arms, the man was able to shove her away. Karin lost her balance and fell to the ground.

"I-I see! This is a trap! High school girls these days . . . I didn't do anything! She threw herself at me! Blackmail me all you like—you'll get nothing!" the man roared, grabbing his golf club and running off into the bushes.

Karin couldn't stand up. She had been shoved onto the ground so fast that it had made her dizzy.

More worrying was that her blood pressure had gotten so high that her mind felt woozy.

As Karin remained where she was on the grass, a slender hand grabbed her shoulder and shook her. "Maaka, what were you doing? Were you trying to get some extra money, hugging men in the park this early in the morning? How crass!"

"N-no . . ."

"No? Then explain exactly what you were doing!"

Karin couldn't.

"See? You can't."

Ayaha snatched her hand away as if she could no longer stand the idea of touching Karin. Her voice was filled with fury and scorn. "Dallying with men for money—exactly like that woman fooling my father. Filthy and despicable. It makes me sick to think there are people like you at my school. Does Usui know—or are you fooling him, too? Or is Usui so poor because you're bleeding him dry?"

Karin didn't answer—but this time, she was physically unable to. *Oh no . . . my blood rush . . . I can't move . . .* Violent waves of unhappiness were pouring out of Ayaha. Karin barely could breath, and her heart was about to explode. All her blood vessels in her body—even in her fingertips and her scalp—were throbbing. Her body temperature was well over one hundred degrees. *Need to . . . bite . . .*

Her vampiric instincts were burning through her brain. She had to expel excess blood. She longed to sink her fangs into a human throat and inject her overflowing blood into it.

"Say something!" someone right next to her yelled.

Karin raised her head, and her eyes locked onto a white throat. Her instincts told her exactly where the vein was. *Ah . . . I can smell . . . unhappiness!* She had lost all reason. Her body had begun to move on its own.

"Wait! What are you doing? Stop!" A shrill voice rattled Karin's eardrums—but the meaning behind the sound never registered. The only thing that did was pleasure—the warmth of the skin against her lips, the feeling of her teeth piercing the skin and sinking into the vein, and the flow of blood past the tips of her fangs. More than anything else, she felt the comfort of her excess blood leaving her body at last.

Karin was moving on pure instinct, and it was hard to say how long she'd remained that way. When she came to again, she scanned the area and found Ayaha Ougimachi lying beneath her, unconscious. There were two holes open on her throat, with vivid red blood trickling from them. "Oh . . . nooo!"

As if Karin's scream were a signal, the bat fluttered down and landed on Ayaha's head, squeaking at her in

a way that made it sound like a warning. Presumably, Anju had seen the entire thing through the bat's eyes.

O-oh, right . . . I should run! Karin thought.

Anju could erase the memories of anyone Karin bit, but if Karin lingered around, all her sister's work would be undone. Karin grabbed her bag and ran for it. *I hope this doesn't lead to trouble. I never imagined I would end up biting Ougimachi. I don't think anyone saw me, but . . .*

Karin's body felt light without excess blood. As she reached the sidewalk, the bat came flying from behind her, flitting around her head. It squeaked, dove into the brush, and flew back to Karin.

"Wh-what? I should go that way?"

The bat flew around her again desperately. Not understanding, Karin left the path, and crouched down in the shadow of the bushes. A second later, the sound of leather soles clomped along the path. Karin stiffened. Still crouching, she peered out at the path. *Kirioka!* She remained still, realizing that he hadn't noticed her.

"Aya? Aya? Where did she go? I could swear I heard her voice coming from this way," Shinobu muttered, irritated. He began walking toward the location where Karin had left Ayaha.

Karin didn't move until Shinobu's footsteps were out of earshot. *That was close. Of all people to almost see me here!* She took a deep breath, forcing herself to calm down, and stepped out of the bushes onto the path. Glancing around herself, she made sure there was no one there, and then broke into a run. She couldn't see the bat anymore. Perhaps it was keeping an eye on Shinobu and Ayaha. *It'll be fine . . . Anju erased Ougimachi's memories, and I hid before he found me,* she told herself, but she couldn't escape the anxiety inside. *I'm probably going to see both of them at school today. Ugh!*

It wasn't Karin's first time seeing people she'd bitten—but when she did, it was always by coincidence. After biting one woman, Karin found out that she was Kenta Usui's mother. Another one ended up working at the same part-time job as Karin, and another ended up transferring to her school. This was her first time biting somebody with whom she knew she would cross paths again. *We're in different grades, so I won't see her that often, but . . . it's still worrying. And the people I bite often end up undergoing dramatic personality changes. What will happen to Ougimachi?* Thinking as she ran, Karin was soon out of breath. *I don't have to run anymore. There are people around now.*

Karin had reached an open grassy area without many trees, where there were people playing with their dogs, exercising together, and mothers out jogging with their babies. She could see other students cutting through the park on their way to school, too. Figuring that running probably would get her noticed, Karin slowed down. *Oh, right . . . I'd better text Anju to thank her.* Reaching for her phone, she exclaimed, "Hey!" The mascot she had attached to her cell phone strap was missing. Maki had given it to her as a souvenir at the beginning of the fall term. It was a leather red fox with its tail in the shape of a K. But now, the fox was missing, and only the strap remained.

Nothing turned up as Karin searched through her bag. *Oh, right—I didn't know when I might have to call Anju, so I put the strap outside the bag so I could get my phone out easily. The string must've broken, and I dropped the fox . . .* Suddenly, Karin's brain froze, and all the blood drained from her face. If she had dropped it, the fox must still be in the place she bit Ayaha. But Ayaha was surely awake by now, and Shinobu probably had found her. If Karin went back to look for the fox, they would suspect her. *I hope I dropped it somewhere else . . .* There was nothing she could do but pray.

Karin left the nature preserve and headed back toward town. Students in the same uniform as she was wearing began increasing in numbers. It had taken some time to find a victim and be found by Ayaha, so Karin was arriving at almost the same time as she usually did. About thirty feet in front of her was a familiar back. That spiky chestnut hair obviously was Kenta's. *Ah, Kenta . . .* Relieved, she could feel the tension drain from her body.

Because Karin was unable to erase memories, attacking and biting someone was a big deal for her. It made her as nervous as taking an exam in her worst subject. This time, her intended victim had run away, and she'd ended up biting Ayaha—someone from her school—and had nearly gotten caught by Shinobu. Then, she realized that she had dropped her mascot. It all added to the stress. But the moment she saw Kenta, all the shrunken blood vessels in her body returned to normal, and her body felt warm and fluffy. *Although I get stressed, if I'm too close to him . . . oh, I should give him today's lunch.* Karin hurried after him, calling out, "Kenta! Good morning. Here . . ."

"K-Karin!" Kenta yelped. Surprised by how loud his own voice was, he took a step sideways and asked in a lower voice, "Are you okay? You looked pretty bad yesterday." It seemed as though Kenta was worried that he would set off Karin's blood rush again. The concern in his eyes and the sweat on his forehead effectively neutralized his naturally intimidating features.

Karin explained quickly, "I'm fine. I bit someone else this morning."

"Who? A stranger?"

Karin hesitated, but she couldn't keep it a secret. Kenta would see the marks on Ayaha's neck and figure it out anyway. "Um . . . Ougimachi."

"Whaaaaaat?" Kenta shrieked.

Karin quickly put her finger to her lips, shushing him, but it was too late. Several girls walking past them already were giggling.

"Lover's quarrel?"

"Isn't it awfully early for that?"

Karin felt her cheeks burning. *I-it isn't like that!*

Kenta scratched his head. "Sorry, you just took me by . . . let's walk while we talk. It's less noticeable."

They started walking. It was a little embarrassing to walk side by side a moment after being mistaken for a couple, but Karin had to explain matters to Kenta.

"Of all people, why Ougimachi? I told you yesterday that Kirioka might suspect something. Why would you go after his cousin? They live in the same house!" exclaimed Kenta.

"It wasn't intentional. I was about to bite somebody else, but . . ." Karin briefly explained how she'd ended up biting Ayaha, and that Shinobu Kirioka had come looking for Ayaha seconds after she'd left the scene, and how she might've dropped a mascot with her initial on it at the scene.

Kenta shook his head. "Why were Ougimachi and Kirioka in the park? They live in the opposite direction."

Karin, obviously, had no idea.

"Anyway, her memories were erased?" asked Kenta.

"Yeah. Anju took care of it. But what should I do if they find the mascot?"

"It doesn't have your name on it—only your initial. And you go through that park twice a day, so you can say you dropped it there some other time. The key is not to appear nervous when you run into either of them. As long as you don't *look* guilty . . ." Kenta glanced down at Karin, adding firmly, "I'll take care of the rest."

A sweet tremble ran through Karin's chest. The dark anxiety that had been about to crush her heart was cleared away by a burst of sunshine. Her voice trembled when she answered, "Th-thank you."

"Don't worry about it. It's what I promised I'd do." Kenta's answer was simple and clear, but somehow lacking.

At that moment, Karin and Kenta heard footsteps running close behind them. Before the pair could turn around, the sweet scent of roses and peaches had enveloped them, and an elegant voice said, "U . . . su . . . i . . . good morning!"

"Gah!" Kenta was pretty strong, and so he was able to avoid being knocked over, but it took him two or three steps to recover from the added weight of the girl now clinging to his back.

Karin's eyes widened, and she froze in her tracks.

The girl who had jumped onto Kenta's back was the same girl Karin had bitten not ten minutes earlier—Ayaha Ougimachi. With her arms wrapped tightly around Kenta's neck and a big smile on her face, Ayaha said, "Hey! You're with Maaka again today? I went to the nature preserve this morning, hoping I could come to school with you, but I guess we missed each other. But I caught you now!"

"O-O-Ougimachi? Wh-what . . . come to school with me? But we live in opposite directions . . ." Kenta seemed flummoxed by Ayaha's overly friendly manner. He managed to twist himself away from her, but he barely could stammer out a response.

As she continued to beam at Kenta, Ayaha cooed, "Aww, you don't need to act so flustered. It's only natural to want to spend more time with the one you love."

"L-l-l-ove?" Kenta whipped backward so fast that his neck almost broke.

Karin was astonished, as well, and stared at the two of them in silence. She had wondered if Ayaha liked Kenta, but a day before, Ayaha had stubbornly refused to admit it. She'd insisted that she'd only wanted to thank Kenta for what he'd done for her after the bike accident—not because she had any feelings for him. But judging by her attitude now . . . *Uggghhh! Because I bit her!* Karin cringed when she realized it was her fault.

Any number of people Karin had injected her blood into had undergone personality shifts as a side effect. Generally speaking, they became more aggressive or more patient—they gained the abilities they needed to overcome the difficulties they were experiencing. *So Ougimachi . . . ends up like this? Right—the first person I bit this summer had a similar reaction. Ugh! What should I do?*

As Karin reeled, Ayaha went right on talking happily to Kenta. "Oh? Why is that a question? I'm talking about you, of course!"

Kenta completely lost the ability to speak. He turned red all the way up to his hairline, and he flapped his mouth like a fish out of water.

They already were close to school. Several students were glancing at them with interest, whispering to each other as they passed. A few even stopped to watch.

"You see, Aya, inexperienced people tend to be uncomfortable talking about such matters in crowded areas," Shinobu sighed, coming up to them with two bags in his hands. "Morning, Usui—Maaka."

"M-mor . . . ning," Karin barely managed to answer. Her head was robotically creaking back and forth from Ayaha to Shinobu, and her eyes had begun to move on their own. Her face went from red to white and back to red again, and her brain had frozen solid. Kenta had warned her to avoid appearing nervous if she'd met either of them, but in a situation like this, how could she possibly keep a level head? Seeing Ayaha with her arms around Kenta was enough to rattle her, and Shinobu's smirk seemed to be hiding so many things that it terrified her.

"If you have enough energy to throw yourself at Usui, carry your own bag, Aya."

"Ah, sorry. But Shino, you didn't say anything! I assumed you didn't mind." Grinning, Ayaha took her bag, turning immediately back toward Kenta. "What—did I over-stimulate you? Maybe I should have built up to it? You mean you've never gone out with a girl before? Oh, well. There's no point in standing around like this. On we go to school!"

As Ayaha spoke, she slid her arm around Kenta's, provoking Kenta to let out a bizarre yelp and jump away. "Eek! N-no . . . um . . . how can I . . . I don't really . . . this is all . . . ah! I'm on a day shift today! I have to run—sorry!" he blathered, offering a nonsensical excuse. Kenta abandoned Karin and Ayaha and ran toward the school. It was clear that he'd completely forgotten about his injured ankle, considering that it was the fastest he'd ever run—far faster than he'd ever run in gym class.

Left behind, Ayaha hung her head and glanced over at Karin. "Usui is so pure emotionally—did you notice? You said you're only a friend, right? Bye." With a slightly superior smile, Ayaha turned to leave.

Karin wasn't breathing. *She knows. She knows perfectly well that I like Kenta!* Yesterday, when Karin had talked to Ayaha in the hall, she had said that she and Kenta were only friends, but Ayaha clearly had seen through that and instinctively recognized their shared feelings—exactly how Karin had suspected that Ayaha was in love with Kenta. *But I can't get close to him!* No matter how much Karin liked him, the deadly combination of her species and her blood rush kept her from ever telling Karin how she felt. Covering her mouth with a clenched fist, Karin hung her head.

Shinobu patted Karin on the shoulder. "Sorry. I don't know what's gotten into Aya today. I've never heard her admit to actually liking someone before."

Karin didn't know how to respond.

"But what Aya calls love is pretty much the same thing a preschooler calls love. And with Usui turning bright red at the very mention of it, she's not going to get very far being aggressive. I don't think you have anything to worry about."

"I-I don't!"

"Personally, I'm more worried about what made her act like this. See you around." Shinobu walked quickly away from Karin, catching up with Ayaha. Whatever he said to her caused her to laugh joyfully.

When Karin finally started walking again, she couldn't help but drag her feet. *Kenta . . . what will he do? What should I do?*

Ayaha had made her intentions perfectly clear. The side effect from Karin's blood would keep her aggressive and honest emotionally for the next month.

Would such a forceful, cheery approach start to move Kenta's heart? And Shinobu—he sounded as though he found Ayaha's transformation suspicious.

Karin's anxieties continued to mount.

By lunch, the skies remained uncommitted. There were heavy gray clouds overhead, but rain had yet to fall.

As always, Kenta took his lunch to the roof and sat on the concrete wall against the fence. He had been going up there by habit, because he used to come to school without any food. But today, he had a better reason. *If I stay in class, Ougimachi might come by . . .* He'd been surprised enough when she'd come by the day before, demanding to buy him lunch—but this morning had been far more shocking. *She "loves" me? Seriously? It isn't some tasteless joke?*

Ayaha had been furious with Kenta two days earlier, when she'd run into him on her bike—but she had taken all the blame for the accident when she'd talked to her cousin and aunt. Then, she'd hurled abuse at him again the next morning—but between classes, she'd kindly offered to buy him lunch. And this morning, Ayaha had thrown her arms around Kenta, smiled broadly, and told him that she loved him. *I don't get it. Is she making fun of me? What for? She didn't seem as though she were lying this morning . . . still . . .*

Kenta never paid much attention to gossip, so he had no idea exactly how popular Ayaha Ougimachi was with the boys at Shiihaba First High. Because of her elegant features and her slim, firm, ballet-trained body, if there were a Miss First High contest, she easily would rank in the top three.

A number of students had seen Kenta and Ayaha that morning—and all day long, Kenta had been fielding accusations and punches from other boys. He'd been getting his hair yanked, his throat throttled, and was repeatedly told to buy the boys lunch.

Considering how quickly Ayaha's attitude toward Kenta seemed to shift, his first instinct was to be suspicious. *Was that a side effect of Karin's blood?* He hadn't spoken to Karin about it yet, because they couldn't afford for that conversation to be overheard. There had been no chance to speak to her alone or to make any plans for how to deal with the matter so far that morning. *What should I do?* His feelings were beginning to resemble the skies. As Kenta munched away at his lunch, he heard the door to the stairs open.

"I thought you'd be here," Ayaha Ougimachi exclaimed happily.

Kenta's knees wobbled, and he almost dropped the lunch from his knees to the ground. He quickly caught it and sat back down.

Without hesitation, Ayaha sat down next to Kenta. "Mind if I eat with you?"

"Wh-why are you here?" asked Kenta.

"Shino told me that you're always here or in the library during lunch."

Kenta made up his mind to hate Shinobu. Unfortunately, he'd only eaten half his lunch. *Avoiding her too obviously would be rude—and she's different every time I see her. I don't know what she wants with me until she actually starts talking.* Kenta was not particularly good at conversations or talking. He had no idea what subjects to introduce, so he put another sautéed green pepper in his mouth.

"You go through the nature preserve twice a day?" Ayaha asked, unwrapping the neatly embroidered cloth from around her lunchbox. "I woke up early and went there, hoping to meet you—but I guess we missed each other. Too bad."

"There are a lot of paths through the nature preserve . . . that's probably why." Ayaha was a year older than Kenta, so he spoke politely.

"Where do you live?"

"Nishi-ku—near Akamagaoka." After Kenta said it, he realized he'd told her too much. He didn't want her coming to his house. But Ahaya appeared to be more interested in the place's name than in Kenta's sudden silence.

"Akamagaoka? I've read that name somewhere, um . . ." Trying to prod her memory, she sketched the kanji in the air with her chopsticks. "That's it!

I saw a book in my father's study. My father runs a land development company. Has anyone asked you to move? Maybe you're outside the area."

"To move? Area for what?"

"There are plans to turn the east side of the hill— the first six blocks of Akamagaoka—into expensive luxury retirement homes. Maybe they haven't started evicting people yet."

"Huh?" The old manor house where the Maaka family lived was on that hill. And Kenta's apartment was on the east side of it. Surprised, his hand shook, and teriyaki meatball slipped from his chopsticks. *Ugh! My precious food!* He caught the meatball with his left hand, popping it directly into his mouth. He had avoided wasting it, but now his hand was sticky.

"Ew, Usui—you're like a child! No, don't put that hand into your pocket—you'll get your clothes dirty. Use this." Amused, Ayaha handed Kenta a handkerchief. It was scented with perfume—the same sweet rose scent that drifted from her hair.

"No, but . . . it'll get dirty."

"I have another one in my locker. You don't need to give it back—I have a bunch more at home," Ayaha said nonchalantly.

The handkerchief appeared to be expensive, and Ayaha had a bunch of them? It was obvious that she'd been brought up with every opportunity. Remembering how his mother's handkerchief was little more than rags, the economic gap between himself and Ayaha burned inside Kenta. But something else was bothering him more. "Sorry. Thanks, I will borrow that . . . but about that land development . . . can you tell me more?"

Ayaha seemed happy that Kenta was interested in something she'd said. She beamed at him and gazed up at the sky, searching her mind for details "Hmm . . . I was flipping through the pages while I was bored waiting for my father, so I don't remember much. But I'm sure it revolved around Akamagaoka, in Nishi-ku. They were going to bulldoze the entire hill and build a one-hundred-thirty-thousand-foot high-priced deluxe retirement home—with a hospital and rehabilitation center, of course—but also a salon and a miniature golf course. The entire thing is designed for rich people."

A plan that extensive would almost certainly involve Kenta's apartment, which was at the base of the hill. He remembered the landlord coming by the room last Saturday. When the man had heard that Kenta's mother was still out looking for work, he'd muttered something about there being no point in telling the child. *Maybe he was going to tell us about the evictions?*

The apartment was thirty years old and had been very cheaply constructed, so the entire building was leaning slightly—and the closet doors didn't shut properly. It hardly could be called a comfortable place to live, but that was exactly why the rent was so cheap. The contract had asked for a guarantor, but they hadn't been particularly picky about it. Because Kenta's mother was unemployed, they were living off his wages. If they were kicked out, they would have nowhere to go. *And it's not only my home—Maaka's place is in trouble, too. Could they find a new home? Or would they refuse to cooperate with the evictions?*

It wouldn't be easy for vampires to find an ideal location for their lair. Naturally, the Maaka family would refuse to move. The development plan would fail, and Kenta and his mother wouldn't need to move. This thought was comforting. *There's no way the land sharks can compete with Karin's parents!* The image of her parents chasing away the land sharks made him smile.

"What? First you're lost in thought, and then you start laughing?" Ayaha asked, frowning at Kenta.

Kenta grimaced, waving a hand. "If people live in the development area, they can't develop it, right? I don't think it'll happen. Karin lives on top of Akamagaoka. I don't think her family would be willing to move."

"On top of Akamagaoka? You're kidding. That's impossible. You must be wrong," Ayaha proclaimed decisively. "The hill and the woods to the east and south are all under city zoning regulation. Nobody lives there."

"Huh? City—?"

"City zoning regulation. It prevents homes from being built at random. Certain areas are designated as non-residential zones. Those zones are for farms or factories, and if you get permission, you can build a retirement home—but not a normal house. I heard my father talking about it at work, so I'm sure," Ayaha explained gravely, obviously not wanting Kenta to think she was making up the story.

Once, before Kenta had known what Karin was, he'd tried to get to her house—but no matter which way he walked, he always ended up back where he'd started, never finding his way to the house. He'd asked Karin later, and she'd explained that there was a barrier in place to keep people from getting close. *Oh . . . people can't get near the mansion. They all think it's an empty hill, with nothing on it but trees.* So, it made sense that someone would attempt to develop it. Kenta's relief dissipated.

When Kenta fell silent again, Ayaha asked in a sulky whisper, "Usui, you know a lot about Maaka. Why is that?"

"W-well, we're in the same class, and we have the same job—so we end up talking a lot."

"Do you like Maaka?"

Kenta almost slammed his face into the lunch on his lap. "Wh-what are saying? We're friends! Only friends."

"Hmm . . . well, what about me?"

"I . . . I don't know how to answer that." Kenta slid sideways, unconsciously trying to put some space between himself and Ayaha. She quickly closed the gap, edging along the wall, being careful to keep her skirt from riding up.

Keeping her gaze fixed on Kenta, Ayaha reminded him, "I told you this morning: I love you, Kenta. Do you hate me?"

"H-hate? No."

"Who do you like better—me or Maaka?"

"I just don't . . . right now, I can't think about loving or hating . . . friends! Both of you are friends, and there are no preferences in friendship!" Kenta's voice reached a near shriek as he was continuously pressed for answers. Covered in sweat, he desperately hoped she would accept his answer.

Ayaha didn't appear satisfied. Her shoulders slumped. "So vague! Could you *not* answer the way Shino said that you would?"

"Huh?"

"He told me that you seemed very inexperienced in matters of the heart, and that I was wasting my time trying to get a clear answer out of you now. He said that you would panic and eventually come out with 'friends.'"

Kenta was exhausted. *Kirioka, if you knew this was going to happen, you could've stopped your cousin!*

Ayaha appeared to have recovered her good humor. "Oh, well. Everything has its time. I guess we'll have to start as friends. Usui, you said Maaka lives on Akamagaoka—but she must be lying. She might be lying about all kinds of other things, so don't be fooled."

Presumably, Ayaha's warning was motivated by simple competitiveness, but it served to remind Kenta. *Oh right, the development plan . . .* The plan was much more important and troubling than whether Kenta liked Karin more than Ayaha. "Can you ask your father for more details about the development plan? My apartment is right up against Akamagaoka. The landlord stopped by the other day, and he might've been there to talk about eviction."

Ayaha frowned, stating awkwardly, "Um . . . I'm not living with him now. I'm living with Shino."

"Oh, yeah. Kirioka said that you were mad at your father."

"I am. It's all my father's fault. I'm not being stubborn or selfish. Really! You can ask Kirioka, if you want." Confident that her actions were justified, Ayaha began to explain exactly why she wasn't living with her father, without Kenta having to ask. "My mother died of kidney cancer last spring, and my father brought his mistress into the house only a year later. He said the house needed a woman's touch. He's an idiot, eating out of that fox's hands. She's obviously only after his money." She bit her lips so hard that they squeaked. "I can't live in the same house as that woman. So, I've been in Shino's house since May. My aunt says I can stay as long as I want—and it's close to school."

The situation didn't make it sound as though Kenta could ask Ayaha to go home and try to get her father to tell her more about the development plan. Discouraged, he fell silent.

Ayaha nodded to herself, brushing her hair back. "Okay, I'll go back one time. That woman might think she's in charge now with me out of the way, so it's worth putting in the occasional appearance. I'm the only woman who has the right to live in the Ougimachi home—not some stupid woman my father picked up on a whim. I'll have to drive that nail home." She really seemed to hate her father's mistress.

Ayaha loudly snapped her lunch box shut, giving Kenta a confident smile. "I have a ballet lesson today, so I can't go by—but I'll swing by home tomorrow after school. If my dad's there, I can't talk to him—but if he isn't, I can look through the documents in his study."

"Y-you won't get in trouble?"

"My father won't be mad. I know he feels guilty about making me move to my aunt's house, so he'll do anything I want him to."

"Could you ask him to cancel the development plans?" Kenta asked genuinely.

Ayaha's smile faded, and she shook her head gravely. "I can't do that. My father's company deals with billions of yen. No matter how much he dotes on me, work is a separate affair. When I was little and my mom was in the hospital, I'd get lonely waiting up late for him to get home, and he always said that all his employees' livelihoods depended on him, so I should forgive him. I'd like to help because *you're* asking me, but I can't do that."

"Oh . . ." Kenta should have known better.

"Dad's worried about me, but the way he shows it is all wrong. He keeps calling and asking if there's anything I want him to buy for me—and he comes by my aunt's house with presents. I'd much rather he kicked that woman out of the house—but he won't say yes to that, which hurts."

Ayaha's father seemed trapped—doting on his daughter but not wanting to break up with his mistress.

"He would rather be with that woman than with me," Ayaha explained. "He never told me that my mother had cancer, and he brought that woman into the house without asking how I felt about it. He doesn't love me nearly as much as he says he does."

Kenta had thought Ayaha was strong-willed and confident, but now her eyes were downcast, and she seemed very lonely. He had no idea how to respond.

Before Kenta had a chance to say anything, Ayaha shook her soft hair. "Yeah, I know I'm being stupid. Aunt Kirioka always wanted a daughter like me, and she loves me like her own—and I have Shino, as well. I'm fine. Anyway, I should look for more information on the Akamagaoka development, shouldn't I?"

"Please. If we know exactly where it is and when they're developing it, it would be a big help. We can't afford to be evicted."

"Ack! Don't bow your head! I'm glad I can help you. I'd be happier if you started to think of me as more than a friend."

Kenta became tongue-tied again.

Ayaha stood up to leave. "I wish I could talk longer, but I still haven't done my math homework. Shino promised to help me, so I'd better go see him. See you later."

Kenta was puzzled that a first year student would be helping a second year student, but Shinobu Kirioka did seem that smart. As he watched Ayaha vanish down the stairs, Kenta realized how tense he'd been. It wasn't until Ayaha was gone that all the muscles in his body relaxed at once. "Ahh . . . what a day." Karin had bitten Ayaha and injected blood into her, and then Ayaha had said that she loved him. Kenta's head was still spinning.

Two days before, when Kenta had crashed into Ayaha, she'd seemed self-centered and difficult to get along with. But now that he'd spoken with her at length, his opinion had changed—she had a softer side. Or was that only because Karin had bit her? *No . . . Karin said that people she bites end up being more like they always wanted to be.*

So, Ayaha's haughty attitude and harsh words over the past couple days had been caused by anxiety over separation from her father, and she had been struggling not to show any of that weakness. *But for as much as she says she loves me, I've never gone out with a girl. My mother's depressed because she can't find a job, and I can't work as much now that school's started again—and there's this development thing. If that's true, we're in trouble.*

Kenta had assumed the Maaka family was invincible because they were full-fledged vampires, but they couldn't move around during the day. Only Karin and her sister could—and if people really became serious about developing the area, they could send the bats out to erase people's memories and alter events only for so long. *I'll have to tell Karin about the development plan.*

Scooping the last few grains of rice out of the lunchbox with his chopsticks, Kenta closed the lid. A raindrop struck the back of his hand. As he looked up at the sky, he noticed that the clouds above were getting darker, and that it had begun to rain.

While Kenta and Ayaha were eating lunch, Maki was furiously questioning Karin.

"Karin, aren't you going to do anything?" asked Maki.

"About what?

"Don't be stupid. About that girl from yesterday! Asako said that the girl told Usui she loved him this morning, and then she hugged and kissed him!"

"N-no, no! Maki, the gossip mill is exaggerating. Ougimachi did jump on Kenta, but she didn't kiss him. I was there."

Because Kenta wasn't in the room, Maki didn't feel the need to beat around the bush. "And you stood and watched? You should push your way between them. Tell Kenta how you feel!"

"I-I won't do that!"

"You make me sick!" Maki rammed her hamburger into her mouth.

Karin tried desperately to defend herself. "Like I said, I really don't have any feelings for him!"

"You're pretending that's true! A shy girl like you . . . finally, you have a boy you actually can talk to. Are you going to let some upperclassman steal a valuable friend like Usui away from you? Sure, Ougimachi might look like a supermodel, but you've got much bigger tits! Have some confidence and go, Karin!"

"Go where? Really, stop this. Kenta and I are only friends—nothing like you think."

"Still," Maki retorted, disgruntled and sucking on her box of coffee milk, "Ougimachi's too much. There are all kinds of other guys, so why'd she have to fall for Usui? Ugh! And I was sure he'd never get any attention, because he's all blunt and scary looking."

"Don't be mean, Maki. Kenta is a little scary looking, but he's really very nice! He never gets angry when I screw things up . . ." Karin had been defending Kenta so passionately that her hand had gotten shaky and she'd dropped a meatball. It bounced off her desk and landed on her chest. "Eek!"

"Ahhh . . . such a waste. Your meatballs are really good." Sighing, Maki picked up the meatball that had fallen to the floor with a tissue. "Karin, every time I say something bad about Usui, you get so worked up that you start dropping food."

"W-well, we're friends, so . . ."

"Now that you have a rival, is this really the time to play around? You have to make up your own mind. Do you really not care if Ougimachi snatches him away?"

Karin ate her sautéed green peppers in silence—but she couldn't taste them at all. She knew Maki meant well by encouraging her, but Karin couldn't admit that she loved Kenta. She couldn't tell him how she felt, because she wasn't human—she was a vampire.

The classroom door opened, and the class vice president, Fukumi Naito, came in. "Hey, Maki, Karin—mind if I eat with you?" she called out.

"Sure. We still have half left."

"Fuku, you were in the teachers' room? Being vice president is so much work," Maki commented, turning an empty chair to line up with their desks.

Fukumi thanked Maki, sitting down with her lunch. "We've received a bunch of requests to use the stage for a play during the cultural festival. We had to tell them to use the classrooms or to do something else. And our class is last in line again. I'll have to bring it up in homeroom. We need to pick something soon."

"There are that many plays?"

"Not only plays—all the clubs are doing stuff, too. The choir and the brass band are—and there's talk of a rock concert. As for the plays, 2-C wants to do a musical. Ayaha Ougimachi's in that class, so they want to make her the heroine and let her dance."

"Huh? What's with her?" asked Maki.

"Don't be like that, Maki. Ayaha's studying classical ballet, and they have great hopes for her, apparently. I heard she performed a short ballet at last year's cultural festival and received thunderous applause." Fukumi gazed at Karin as she spoke in a way that implied that she'd heard the rumors about Kenta and Ayaha.

Karin hung her head.

"According to a second year student in my club, people are always asking Ayaha out. She's beautiful, but she grows tired of people quickly and famously has never gone out with anyone for long. She usually dates someone for about a week. I heard that Ayaha is excited about someone again right now, but given her personality, she'll lose interest soon." It was obvious Fukumi was telling Karin not to worry, but it only made Karin hang her head more.

"I hate girls like that," Maki fumed. "If you're going to get bored that quickly, don't go out with guys in the first place! Ayaha's lucky she hasn't gotten herself a stalker or worse. That would make her learn her lesson."

Fukumi grimaced. "Ayaha has her cousin, Shinobu. If anyone does anything strange, he takes care of it."

"Takes care of it? Kirioka's the president of B class, right? With the glasses, he looks more like a literature major—not like the fighting type." Maki knew Kirioka's name and face only, and appeared surprised that he was such a protector.

Fukumi's grimace deepened. "That's only what Shinobu looks like. He's a lot more twisted than he appears."

Karin's heart began beating quickly. Kenta had warned her yesterday that Shinobu might be suspicious of her true nature. But neither of them really knew much about Ayaha's cousin. "What do you mean by twisted, Fuku?" Karin asked.

"We're both on the student council, so we see each other at meetings. Normal methods don't work with Shinobu. If he's on your side, it's great—but you don't want him working against you. A third year student took issue with his opinion at one meeting and got ripped to pieces. And," Fukumi lowered her voice, "any boys that have hung around Ayaha, or girls that have been angry because she stole their boyfriends . . . they all suddenly get very quiet. If you ask them why, they'll never tell you—but it sounds as if Shinobu's behind it."

The more Karin heard, the more worried she became. If someone like Shinobu suspected what she was . . . and this morning, she'd bitten Ayaha. What would Shinobu think when he saw the marks on Ayaha's throat?

When Fukumi saw Karin fall silent, she realized she'd probably said too much. "That's merely a rumor. Nobody's been physically hurt. Shinobu might be a bit weird, but nothing's going to happen to Kenta. He'll be fine."

"Mmm . . ." Karin uttered. Apparently, Fukumi thought she was worried about Kenta—which made sense, considering Kenta was the only human who knew that Karin was a reverse vampire. Even her best friend Maki didn't know. Neither Maki nor Fukumi ever would have guessed that Karin was afraid her identity might be discovered. *Kenta and Ougimachi . . . and Kirioka might do something mean to Kenta . . . and he might know what I am. Why does all this have to happen at once?* Karin sighed, feeling overwhelmed.

She closed her empty lunchbox. Maki and Fukumi were done eating, as well. "I'd better go wash my necktie," Karin said, glancing down at the teriyaki sauce in the spot that the meatball had landed. She had to get it off before it stained.

On Karin's way to the bathroom, she saw Kenta coming toward her. When he saw her, he looked relieved. "Karin, I was looking for you on my way to class."

"For me?" asked Karin, surprised. *We'd see each other in fifth period, anyway*, Karin thought, cocking her head.

Kenta quickly scanned the area and said in a low voice, "I was eating lunch with Ougimachi on the roof."

Karin's heart skipped a beat. While she'd been bearing up under Maki's onslaught, Kenta had been with Ayaha. Which one of them had suggested eating together? Kenta had run away this morning, so it must have been Ayaha's idea. *But they did eat together, so he didn't turn her down . . .* That hurt. Karin barely could stand to look at Kenta and hung her head—but the next thing Kenta said drove all such thoughts out of her mind.

"Ougimachi's dad's company is doing some land development. They're talking about bulldozing the hill your house is on."

"Whaaa—?"

"According to the official documents, nobody lives on Akamagaoka. She says they're going to build a huge luxury retirement home in place of the hill, including my apartment."

"Th-then . . . my family . . . and yours . . ."

"We're going to be evicted."

"Noooooo!" This was one too many things to think about. Karin's brain short-circuited, and smoke poured out her ears.

The only illumination in the vast dining room was a single table lamp. The corners of the room and the high ceiling were shrouded in darkness.

Normal vampires could see in the dark and didn't need artificial light. The light was for the benefit of Karin's unusual nature, and for Kenta, who was human.

Knowing more information about the land development was critical. It affected the Maaka family's very survival. Karin decided to bring Kenta with her after work, instead of relaying things second hand and getting the details wrong.

"Bulldoze the entire hill to build a retirement home? Why do humans love development so much?" Calera moaned.

Henry clutched his temples. "Usui is right—this is not a residential zone. They can't build normal houses here."

"But you actually do live here. The building's pretty old . . . wasn't any paperwork done?" Kenta asked, glancing around at the shadowy ceilings and antique fireplace.

"It was built in the Meiji era," Henry replied. "After our family crossed over to Japan, we began looking for a place to settle down and discovered it. It was far more decayed at first."

The state of the building was a blessing in disguise, it seemed. Supposedly, it was considered haunted at one time, so nobody went near it. After the vampires had started living in it, they had gradually repaired it, making it fit for habitation. For safety's sake, they'd placed a barrier at the base of the hill, preventing people from drawing near. Eventually, people forgot the building had ever been there, and grew to believe the hill was entirely covered in trees.

"Then came the Second World War. Shiihaba had been bombed fairly heavily, but this hill remained safe. After the war, the surviving areas and the burned lands were reevaluated, and new zoning areas were created— but nobody remembered there was a mansion on this hill. Because there was nothing here but hills, it wasn't designated as a residential zone."

"But Dad, we get water and electricity in spite of the fact there's no house here officially," Karin noted.

"The gas and electric companies don't bother to check what zone you're in. They simply do the construction when you ask them."

"We should've leeched a line, and then we wouldn't have to pay for it," Ren snorted.

Calera glared at Ren. "Amateurs couldn't do construction for an electric or gas line. A vampire electrocuting himself? The shame!"

"And using gas and water without permission is theft. Vampires have too much pride to do something like that!" Henry noted.

Calera nodded in agreement before sighing and returning to the subject at hand. "As this wasn't a residential district, we avoided attention from speculators during the bubble economy, but now . . ."

"Couldn't you get it officially recognized as our land retroactively? Alter the memories of the civil servants in charge and have them draw up the proper documents? If it's our private property, the developers would have to give up," Ren concluded with glittering eyes. He appeared to be ready to fly off and do it immediately.

Calera shook her head, pitying her son's naivety. "Don't be stupid, Ren. The office closes at five o'clock. There's a month before the sun starts setting in time, and by then, it'll be too late."

"If this required nothing more than the seduction of a few women, we'd certainly leave things in your hands, Ren—but that's impossible. We'd have to change it from a non-residential district to a residential district before we could do anything else—and that's not going to happen by getting a few people on our side," Henry stated plainly. "And Ren, you're forgetting something important."

"What's that, Dad?" asked Ren.

"If we register the land, we have to pay taxes."

"Urp."

"And the tax office checks people very thoroughly. Talking about taxes could quickly lead to the matter of citizenship and birth certificates. More and more people would get involved. Soon, it would be well beyond a level that could be handled by manipulating memories, and much harder than faking the paperwork needed to attend public school."

"So, what can we do?" shrieked Ren.

Listening to the vampires argue, Kenta whispered to Karin: "Your entrance forms were faked?"

"Yeah, we don't have a birth certificate or proof of citizenship," replied Karin.

"Oh. That makes things tough."

"But we're not human, so there isn't anything else we can do."

"I can't do anything about birth certificates or anything official, but if there's anything I can do to help with school, please say so. You don't have to handle everything yourself."

Karin hung her head, certain she was blushing at the concern in Kenta's voice.

"Something wrong, Karin?"

"N-no, nothing." Karin's feelings for Kenta meant that almost anything he said could make her happy or could make her turn red—but she couldn't tell him that. She picked up the cup from the table in front of her and pretended to take a sip of tea.

There were only two cups on the table. Karin had quickly made them for herself and Kenta, feeling that it would be rude not to, considering he'd come all this way. Anju said she wasn't thirsty, and her parents never drank human beverages.

Suddenly, Henry turned toward Karin and Kenta. "Usui."

"Yes?"

"This girl, the land development company president's daughter. She told you about the plan because she has affection for you?"

"A-affection? That might be a side effect of the blood Maaka . . . Karin injected into her."

"If you have time to be embarrassed, please answer the question," Calera snapped. "This development plan is far more important. The question is whether this girl is on your side."

"Apparently so. She's been arguing with her father and is living with her aunt right now—but she promised to swing by her house tomorrow to try to find out when development will begin, and the exact area affected," Kenta replied in one breath. It seemed as though he'd made himself thirsty, because he took a big gulp of tea afterward.

Maybe I should've made it stronger. I wonder how Kenta likes it? I put milk in it because we were out of lemon. I hope he likes it that way, Karin thought, taking a sip of tea. Her thoughts were focused on all the wrong things.

Ren leaned back in his chair, glared at the ceiling, and whispered, "Boy, make that woman your bitch, so she'll go crying to her father, begging him to stop the plan."

Karin and Kenta simultaneously spit out their tea and coughed.

Calera covered her eyes with one hand. "Ren, are you physically unable to use more refined language? Your sisters are so much younger . . . Do you really believe this boy could manipulate a girl's heart in that way? You'd have a better chance."

"Me? Please. No woman Karin bit would ever whet my appetite," insisted Ren. "She's all fired up now, without a trace of stress, right?"

"Either way, it wouldn't lead to anything. A plan on this scale has billions of yen backing it. No matter how hard his daughter cries, the father's hardly going to abandon it," Calera said.

Between coughs, Kenta nodded. "Y-yeah. I did ask Ougimachi if she'd try to make her father stop, but she said he wouldn't listen to her if it involved his work."

Henry smirked. "I thought as much."

"This is no time to stroke your beard proudly, Dad. What the hell can we do?" Ren asked again, irritated.

Suddenly, Anju, who'd been listening in silence, stood on her feet. She walked to the wall and opened the window. The sound and smell of rain, and a wave of chilly air drifted into the room.

"What is it, Anju?" asked Calera.

Anju turned around, disregarding her mother, and peered at Karin and Kenta, both of whom were still coughing. "Someone followed you. Someone's been wandering around the barrier since you arrived."

Karin's parents and brother glared at the sisters.

Using her bats to search outside, Anju began describing the interloper. "He has a gray checked umbrella, a black shirt, and jeans. He's in high school, maybe, and is about five foot six, with black hair and glasses."

"That's Kirioka—Shinobu Kirioka—from our school. He's in B class, which is different than ours," Karin explained.

But Karin and Kenta had been working at Julian until eight. They hadn't come to Karin's house directly from school, so why was Shinobu wandering around the vicinity?

"A lot of people know Karin and I work at Julian. If someone wanted to, he could watch outside the restaurant and wait for us to go home to follow us," Kenta groaned.

"I doubt Kirioka came here by accident," Anju whispered. "He had a map with him. He's checking his direction against the lights in the town below—and he's noticed that no matter how straight he thinks he's walking, he ends up somewhere else. The only reason the barrier caught him is because he was following at a distance to avoid being noticed. You were lucky."

The scathing edge to Anju's voice made Kenta shift his eyes awkwardly. "I knew Kirioka was suspicious of Karin, but I didn't think he'd follow her."

"It isn't your fault! I didn't see him, either," exclaimed Karin.

"It doesn't matter—we'll have to erase Kirioka's memories," Ren insisted, raising a hand, presumably to command the bats flitting around the edges of the barrier.

"Wait! Kirioka isn't someone who can be dealt with lightly," Kenta yelled. "He's the kind of guy who probably would write down all the information he's uncovered."

Ren lowered his hand, vexed.

Henry frowned, stroking his beard. "That's bad. If we erase his memory here, and he goes home and finds a note to himself, he'll grow more suspicious."

"Ah . . . he's leaving. It seems as though he's decided there was no point in walking any farther," Anju whispered.

The rain grew louder. No sooner had Anju closed the window than Ren's irritation burst out of him. "Karin, why the hell did you bite someone related to the guy who's already suspicious of you? Now he's even more suspicious, and he's following you around!"

"Ugh! I'm so sorry!" Karen groaned.

"Sorry won't solve shit! The land development thing is trouble enough—and if someone finds out where we live . . ." Ren shouted.

"Calm yourself, Ren. There isn't anything to be gained by yelling at Karin now. We have to concentrate on what to do," Calera asserted soothingly, propping her cheek on one hand. She glanced over at Kenta and Karin. "We need more information, both about the development project and about this boy Kirioka. Let me see . . . Usui?"

"Y-yes?" Kenta answered in a stiff voice, shivering. The last time he'd been to Karin's house, they'd all intimidated him. He was already more than a little scared of Calera.

"Ougimachi said she would go home tomorrow to ask about this development plan, right? What do you think about going with her?" Calera proposed.

"M-me?"

"Yes. We want the information as direct and as accurate as possible. You're in danger of being evicted, too, so the development plan also affects you."

"True, but—"

"Then, go home with Ougimachi, and ask the company president yourself."

"B-but will Ougimachi let me come with her?"

"Of course she will. I'd bet money on it. And don't only look for details—see if there's any possibility of making the company abandon its plans. If it's still at a stage where only the president and his secretaries know about the development plan, we might be able to make them forget it entirely."

"But if Ougimachi knows, that means the plan's probably pretty well known."

"So, find out for sure! Or are you refusing to help us?"

"N-no! Never!" Kenta vowed, terrified.

Karin sat glumly beside Kenta. *Kenta will spend all afternoon with Ougimachi tomorrow.* Karin knew her mother's idea was a good one. It was the best way to find out more about the development plan, and it wasn't as though she and Kenta were dating—they were friends. Karin had no right to complain if Kenta spent time with another woman. But the idea of it pained her.

"Karin. Hey, Karin! Are you listening? This is no time to zone out!" Calera exclaimed.

"Wh-what, Mama?" Karin asked, trying to fake a smile as she glanced up.

Calera scowled at her disoriented daughter. "Forget it. You'd never pull it off."

"Mama! Don't say that, especially without telling me what you wanted!"

"I was going to suggest that you try to find out exactly how much Kirioka knows—but you can't, can you?"

Karin's family responded before she could get a word in edgewise.

"Karin? No, never!"

"Impossible."

"Mother, that's asking a bit much."

"I think it would make things worse."

"H-how mean . . ." Karin whimpered, getting abuse from all directions. She slumped against the table.

Joanna, the doll in Anju's arms, dealt the finishing blow: "It isn't anything to be shocked by anymore, surely. Everyone knows how clumsy you are." This particular doll wasn't quite as rude as Boogie, but its words were venomous, regardless.

Anju left the window and sat down in her chair. "That boy outside went past twice, realized something was wrong, went by another time carefully watching his direction, and left after he was sure he was being forcibly misdirected. His concentration powers are very strong, and he has the judgmental ability to avoid wasting time. Compare that to Kenta's ability. When Kenta got caught in the barrier, he went around about ten times before giving up in exhaustion."

Kenta's face reddened at the thought that he was being chided for qualities he lacked.

Ignoring Kenta's obvious embarrassment, Anju continued dissuading Karin. "Kirioka isn't someone you can handle. Odds are that he'll get you by the tail and push you to the edge of the cliff. Try to avoid him, if you can."

Karin moaned, unable to defend herself against the relentless wave of sense.

Ren snorted. "What, did you *want* to spend time with Kirioka?"

"N-no! Don't say weird things!" Karin could feel steam rising from her face. *How could Ren say that with Kenta around? I don't want to spend time with Kirioka! Both Fuku and Anju made him sound so smart that it was scary.* Karin also was embarrassed to have her whole family dismiss her as useless in front of Kenta. Kenta knew full well what Karin was, but she didn't want him to think she was so clumsy that he started to hate her. She knew they were different species and that their love could never be. *But I want to stay friends at the very least.*

Eventually, the conversation concluded. Kenta would go with Ayaha the next day to find out more information. Kenta and Karin's family would formulate a plan based on the findings.

Karin escorted Kenta to the door. "Sorry, Kenta. My mother's a little bossy."

"Don't worry about it. I'm in as much danger of eviction as you are. I'll ask Ougimachi and get that information."

Every time Kenta said Ayaha's name, it felt like a needle stabbing Karin in the heart. Karin had been wondering what Kenta thought of Ayaha, and the words started tumbling out. "S-she's . . . really pretty. Her father's a company president, and she studies ballet. She's practically the perfect girl."

Kenta thought about it. "Well, Ougimachi's certainly not lacking for money—but her mother's dead, and her father has a mistress living in the house, so it isn't all happy. If you hadn't bitten her and given her a power boost, she probably never would have agreed to go home."

"I suppose," Karin muttered.

"She tends to shift a lot, which I find hard to deal with—but she's nicer than I originally thought. She seems to want to help, so I think she'll come through. Karin, you have to make sure Kirioka doesn't grow any more suspicious."

"Yeah . . ."

"No matter what he asks, simply say that you don't know or don't remember. See you tomorrow." Kenta went out into the rain, huddling under a battered old umbrella.

Karin retreated to her room, flopping down on the bed and sighing heavily. Kenta had said that Ayaha was hard to deal with, but he'd also called her nice. Which impression won out? And which impression would grow stronger the more he got to know her? *Kenta . . .*

There was a gentle knock on Karin's door. Anju peeked in, clutching Joanna. "Dinner, Karin?"

"Ah . . . there's yesterday's salad and cream stew in the fridge," Karin replied.

"I saw it, but there was only one serving."

"You eat it. I'm not hungry," Karin said, staring at the ceiling. The heaviness she felt on her chest left her with no appetite. *Kenta's getting closer and closer to Ougimachi.* Tears welled up from behind Karin's eyelids, even when she closed them. She turned sideways, burying her face in her pillow, utterly terrified to face the morrow.

As the evening sky turned tangerine, the bell rang, signaling the end of homeroom.

"Be careful going home!" urged Shirai, the homeroom teacher. After he left, the students began moving quickly.

Karin gathered her things, sighing unconsciously. Maki had started for the door, but she turned around, making her way to her best friend. "Karin, you're sighing again. What's with you today? Are you feeling sick?"

"Nothing like that. I'm fine, really. I was in gym, right?"

"Yeah, you were . . . but you don't seem like yourself. Maybe you should take a breather in the nurse's office before you head home."

"No, no—I have work today."

"You should get Usui to walk with you. He's working today, right?" Maki asked, beaming as if the idea were absolutely genius. She looked around for Kenta, but Karin quickly stopped her.

"No, no, no! Kenta isn't working today."

"Aw! Did he already leave? That was fast. Okay, though—I get it," Nodding several times, Maki leaned in and whispered, "You're all glum because you can't work with Usui today. Why didn't you say so?"

"No! Please stop connecting everything to Kenta! I have to go. I'll be late to work." Karin quickly bolted out of the room. She was sure Maki would figure out the truth otherwise. *Kenta's going with Ougimachi to her house today . . .*

Apparently, Ayaha had gone to the roof to eat with Kenta again today. She'd mentioned wanting to get her fall and winter clothes while she was there, and Kenta had managed to get himself invited along to help carry baggage. He didn't tell Karin until much later.

Kenta had left the classroom the second homeroom ended, heading for 2-C to meet Ayaha. They had to be heading home by now. Ayaha was so outgoing that she'd told Kenta she loved him in front of everyone. What could they be talking about, and what was it like for Kenta to spend time with her? No matter how many times Karin drove thoughts like these out of her mind, they crept back. Buffeted by waves of anxiety,

Karin had managed to make her way to the shoe lockers when she heard a voice.

"Hello, Maaka," a familiar voice rang out from behind her. Karin jumped. When she turned hesitantly around, she saw Shinobu Kirioka standing behind her, smiling. "Shall we walk home together?"

"Hmm? Kenta said you live in Amemiya-shi? I'm in the opposite—"

"But you're working at the restaurant today, aren't you? I heard you run out of the classroom shouting that you're going to be late. I have some errands to run, and I'm going that way, too," Shinobu said, silencing Karin's protests without blinking an eye. He changed from his slippers into a pair of black leather shoes and kept prodding. "Weren't you in a hurry?"

"Ah . . . er . . . um . . ."

"If you really don't want to walk with me, fine. But in that case, I'd at least like to know what I did to make you hate me. Should I ask Usui? He seems to get along with you. I found his house yesterday, so I can ask him any time."

Karin's legs trembled. If she ran away, Shinobu would take it out on Kenta. *I can't cause Kenta any more trouble,* she thought. Kenta was going to Ayaha's house today mostly because Karin's mother had forced him to. If Karin directed Shinobu's attention toward Kenta, as well, she could never bear to face him again.

Shinobu waved. "Bye then, Maaka."

"Wait!"

"Thought so," Shinobu added, grinning. It seemed as though it were a completely innocent smile, but the light glinted off his glasses, hiding his eyes.

As the pair walked toward the gate together, Karin had no idea what to say.

Shinobu spoke first: "Your eyes are an unusual color, Maaka. Most Japanese people have brown irises, but yours have a hint of red—or garnet. It's like you're from another country."

"Y-yeah, my parents are . . ." Karin started; she almost continued with, "from another country," but she stopped herself. Kenta had told her not to say anything to Shinobu except for, "I don't know" and "I don't remember." It was too late now.

"Oh, they aren't Japanese? I thought not. Maaka's an unusual name. Do you have relatives abroad? Do you keep in touch with them?"

"No . . . we're not in touch anymore. I've never heard anything about them."

"Oh, what a shame. I'm curious about other cultures. I'm thinking about studying abroad after high school—or at least my cousin is. She wants to study ballet in Europe, so I've been trying to get a little more information. Aya can't be bothered with things like that. She's passionate about what she loves, and she works really hard at it—but everything else just slips past her."

Remembering what—or who—Aya was passionate about at the moment, Karin grew maudlin.

"Say, if your parents are from another country, they must follow some of their old customs, right? Would you mind if I visited your house sometime?"

All the talk of studying abroad had been leading up to this—a justifiable reason to investigate the vampires' lair. Without hesitating, Karin shook her head. "Never!"

"Why not? Usui's been there, hasn't he?"

"Kenta knows, so he's special. *Ugh!*"

"Special how? Knows what?"

"Uh . . . um . . . we live near each other! We see each other a lot. I can't bring anyone else, because my dad would be furious!" Putting all the blame on her father, Karin desperately tried to work her way out of the sticky situation.

Shinobu slumped his shoulders. "Oh, well. I'd like to see your house . . . find out what kind of people your family members are. You didn't tell me which country your parents are from, did you? Judging from your face and hair, and the color of your eyes, I assume it's not Asia or Africa? America . . . no. Europe? Black hair tends to indicate the south and east, I think. Am I right?"

"Um, they've never said."

"You don't know what your nationality is?"

Deflecting one blow after another, Karin stuck to her guns. "I don't know."

"Your own nationality?"

"I've never really thought about it."

"I suppose it isn't something that affects daily life. Maybe Usui knows?"

"This has nothing to do with him!"

"But you said it yourself: He's special."

"I-I didn't mean anything by that!"

"Reeeaaallly? It sounded like you did."

They had only walked the short distance from the school to the gate, but Karin was already exhausted. *Oh god, I want to be alone.*

Unfortunately for Karin, Shinobu had been waiting to get out of earshot of the other students before beginning his real questions. As they walked down the street, past trees with their leaves starting to change color, he began firing arrows at her once again. "You live in Nishi-ku, in Akamagaoka, right? I checked the address book. You live in the first block—no, the second, right? I was under the impression that area wasn't a residential zone, but was I wrong about that?"

"I . . . I really don't know about those things."

"Probably not. Maybe the address book is wrong. I tried to go to your house yesterday, but I never found it."

Karin barely managed to stop herself from saying, "I know." Instead, she quickly forced herself to say, "Wh-wh-what for?"

"No reason. I was in the area and thought I'd stop by—but I ended up getting lost."

"R-really?"

"I've never once been lost as long as I've had a map. It was as if some weird trick was preventing me from going straight. No matter how carefully I walked, I always ended up back where I started. If this were some occult TV show, it would've been called a mystery zone. Maybe I should call one of those shows and have them film there."

"Oh god, don't! If that happened . . . !" Karin shrieked. There was a limit to how well the bats could maintain the barrier—especially during the day, when only Karin's sister was awake. Keeping up a strong barrier to drive away a persistent TV crew would utterly exhaust Anju.

Shinobu smirked. "If that happened . . . what? Problems?"

Karin couldn't answer. If she made up a weak excuse, Shinobu would catch it and dig even deeper. "Not that I'd really call a TV show. I'm not bored enough to answer their questions."

Karin slumped. *Then, don't suggest it . . .*

The two of them probably came off as a couple of friendly students walking and talking—an everyday occurrence—but Karin's neck and back were soaked with sweat. They passed beneath a traffic signal, and the two-lane road turned into a one-lane street. There were fewer cars as a result, and almost no one else was around.

"When I point things out like this, there ends up being a lot of strange things about you," Shinobu muttered. "You live somewhere you aren't supposed to live, where nobody can get to, and your nationality is a mystery. Did you know it's easy enough to peek at the citizenship registries if you put your mind to it? I'll have to go down to city hall and check it out. If you really do live where the address book says you do, I should find out some interesting things."

Karin was almost frothing at the mouth now. Shinobu could forget confirming her address—she wasn't registered at all. "No! That's an invasion of privacy!"

"If you'd tell me the truth, I wouldn't have to go to all that trouble."

The truth? The strength of the term made her stiffen.

The friendly smile had vanished from Shinobu's face. He reached into his pocket and held up something dangling from a string that he twirled in the air. It was a red fox made of leather.

"Ah!" Karin cried, clapping her hands over her mouth and wincing. Having reacted the way she did, Karin realized that she'd revealed both that she recognized the fox and that there was something sinister behind it.

The coldness in Shinobu's gaze grew more pronounced. "You've seen this before. I found it next to Aya in the nature preserve yesterday morning. She was unconscious. I asked a girl in D class, and she recognized it instantly as something that both Tokitou and Maaka had hanging from their cell phone straps. Tokitou's was still on her strap—and the letter K obviously stands for either Karin or Kenta . . ."

"Th-that does belong to me, but I don't know where I dropped it."

"Please, stop with the transparent excuses—you'll only make me mad. Aya was lying on the ground and this was on top of her skirt. Do you mean to suggest that you found Aya lying there, got close enough to drop the fox, and then went away, leaving her there?"

Karin couldn't think of a believable story.

"And don't try to pretend you dropped the charm somewhere else and someone picked it up and put it on top of Aya. It was raining two days ago, and the ground in the park was still wet. Leather soaks up moisture, but this was bone dry. You ran into Aya there, did something to her, and dropped it."

"Um, um, I didn't do—"

"Don't lie to me. It would save a lot of time if you told me everything."

Karin couldn't think of a way out of the bind. Her legs trembled, and she was covered in sweat. She knew the more nervous she acted, the more certain Shinobu would become—but she couldn't stop herself. *What should I do? What should I do? What . . .* At this rate, Karin was dancing in the palm of Shinobu's hand. *I can't deflect his questions any longer!*

Karin spun around, planning to run down the side alley, but Shinobu grabbed her shoulder. "Ugh!" She tried to get away, but to her surprise, Shinobu didn't pull her backward. Instead, he used her momentum and pushed her into the alley. "Eek!" She stumbled—but this time, he did pull. Karin reeled backward, slamming her back against the wall. Hearing a slapping sound right next to her face, she ducked. When she opened her eyes again, Shinobu was standing with his hand against the wall, blocking her escape.

"Maaka, honestly—I really don't like having to be this forceful. I'm getting angry, though. Depending on your reactions, I might have to get rough." Despite the frigid gleam in his eyes, his tone was conversational and completely ordinary, which made him even more frightening. "No matter how you look at it, Aya's acting strange. People get the wrong idea about her, because she sounds haughty or stuck up—but that's not the real her. It's all a bluff—an act to hide the fragile girl inside."

Karin didn't move a muscle, keeping her back pinned against the wall, listening.

"Yesterday morning, Aya left the house earlier than usual. She said that it was her turn to help get the lab ready for her first period biology class. My mother offered to drive her if she would wait a minute longer, but Aya refused, which isn't like my spoiled cousin at all. I thought something was up, so I followed her. She didn't go to school at all—she went to the nature preserve."

"Ah . . ."

"She'd lied to me and my mother—but when she met Usui, she had no problems admitting that she'd wanted to walk to school with him. And she did it in front of a big crowd, which she would never usually do."

Shinobu had lost sight of Ayaha while dodging an angry dog, and when he'd found her again, she was lying defenseless on the ground. Only five or ten minutes had passed from the time he'd first seen her until the time he shook her awake. "Something happened during those few minutes, right?" Something that could transform Ayaha's personality into one more confident, aggressive, and unafraid of failure. Shinobu peered directly into Karin's eyes. "Aya might be a coward, but she's also very proud. She's afraid of being embarrassed and rejected, and that prevents her from saying how she really feels. She always acts as though people should feel privileged that she allows them to be her friends. But the way she acted with Usui yesterday . . . What did you do to her?"

Karin shook her head but said nothing. There were people walking by on the street outside, but none of them looked toward her. If someone had, she and Shinobo undoubtedly would have been mistaken for a couple, because they were in their uniforms. No one would come to save her. *What should I do? Kirioka's really angry—but I can't tell him that I bit her and injected my blood into her!* Tears welled up, blurring her vision.

"*Tch!* You think crying will get you out of this? As I said, I'm really angry. The more you suck up to me, the madder I'll get. You should have fixed yourself before you tried personality alteration on Aya."

"Personality alteration?" Karin exclaimed, feeling as though the phrase sounded particularly sinister.

"That's what you did, isn't it? Brainwashing—like they talk about cults doing? Argh! I don't have time to mince words. I'm going to tell you my theory: Maaka, you're an illegal immigrant, aren't you? And you're squatting in the non-residential zone."

Karin gaped at Shinobu. It was true that her family had come here without passing through immigration offices; so technically, it was fair to call them immigrants. But Shinobu was obviously way off.

"I don't know how you made me lose my way near your house, but it was probably something to do with sound waves distorting my sense of balance. Or perhaps you used the flatness of the terrain to create the effect of highway hypnosis."

"Highway . . . what?"

"You've heard how people claim they saw a ghost on the highway at night, right? That happens when they're driving past unchanging landscape and get sleepy. They end up driving in a state somewhere between sleep and awake. But seeing as you're doing it, why am I explaining this to you? Stop trying to play innocent."

"B-but I really don't know!"

"You're a surprisingly good actor. It seems too elaborate a defense if all you have to hide is being illegal immigrants, so you must be smuggling in other people from your country—or smuggling drugs."

"Drugs?" Karin shrieked. If her proud father knew his family was being accused of such a base crime, he'd explode with fury. When he'd been mistaken for a peeping Tom near the end of the summer, he'd beaten the actual criminal until his face had doubled in size. Karin herself was offended.

"Don't raise your voice, Maaka. You're the one who doesn't want this getting out, right?"

"B-but it's not true!"

"I don't expect you to admit it."

"I swear! We're not doing anything criminal! We're just vampires. *Eeek!*" Karin had been so focused on her denial that she'd blurted out the truth. She turned pale, covering her mouth with her hands.

All Shinobu did was sneer. "Is that supposed to be funny? Surely you can think of a better lie than that."

"Er . . . um . . ."

"What's next? You came from outer space? We can skip all the tall tales. Why don't you tell me the truth before I get really angry?"

Unbeknownst to Karin, Shinobu was a committed realist. He took her slip as merely a bad lie, breezing right past it.

Ah . . . but how can I explain why Ougimachi's personality changed? Karin wondered. If Shinobu refused to admit that vampires could exist, she couldn't tell him the truth if she wanted to. He never would believe her.

Karin's silence seemed to infuriate Shinobu, and his voice grew frosty. "Honestly, I don't give a damn what your family is doing as long as it has nothing to do with me. I just want to know what you did to Aya and what effect it's going to have on her. Was it some kind of personality alteration? Surely that takes time. Hypnotism? If you used some sort of drug that's going to do permanent damage . . ." Shinobu took his hand off the wall and pushed his glasses up his nose. There was a dangerous look in his eyes that made Karin tremble.

"No, no! She'll be back to the old Ougimachi in about a month," Karin insisted. "I never would use anything so scary!"

"One month? How specific. What did you do? Aya doesn't remember what happened to her. If what you did was legitimate, there's no reason to hide it. It must have been something you can't afford to have her remember, seeing as you made her forget—which means it's time to stop playing around." Shinobu grabbed Karin's left hand by her thumb.

"Ooow!" Karin yelped. Shinobu had twisted her hand backward, sending a wave of pain up her arm. The bag she'd been holding fell to the ground.

"If Aya had wanted it, that's fine—but that's not how it happened, is it? Whatever the reason, changing someone's personality against her will is unforgivable! Tell me what you did to her, and what it's doing to her! It might be your left hand, but if your thumb won't move, it'll make things hard for you!"

"Stop! Ow! Stop!"

Shinobu's face and voice were flat and cold, and never revealed how furious he really was. But the way he was calmly about to break Karin's thumb was terrifying. Tears flowed down her cheeks.

"Why Aya? Why not someone else? Revenge for her trying to steal Usui?"

"No, nothing like that!" Trying to free her hand from Shinobu's grasp, Karin shook her head violently. Her hair whipped around, sending her tears flying in all directions.

"It wasn't deliberate! I didn't mean to!" Karin's heart hurt more than her finger. She honestly had not meant any harm by biting Ayaha. She was a reverse vampire, and her blood rush had reached its limit. Ayaha Ougimachi had accidentally ended up in front of her, and that was it. "*Sniff* . . . uuuggghhh!" Karin's self-control snapped, and she burst into tears.

Ayaha's personality had changed as a side effect of Karin's blood, so it definitely was the reverse vampire's fault. But that wasn't what Karin had wanted. After all, it was Karin who was in trouble now that Ayaha was pursuing Kenta so aggressively.

Thoughts of remorse cluttered Karin's mind. *I . . . I never wanted to be a blood-injector. I wanted to be a normal vampire like Mom, Dad, and my brother . . . Then, I wouldn't have to bite people blindly when my blood rush grew too intense!* And Karin never would've accidentally bitten a student at her school—someone she saw all the time—nor would she have aroused Shinobu's suspicions like this. No longer thinking straight, Karin began to babble. "I . . . I never wanted . . . to be born like . . . *sniff* . . . like this. I wanted to be like . . . like Mom and Dad . . . *sniff* . . . *sob* . . . uuuggghhh!" Her words separated by sobs, she barely said anything comprehensible—which was probably a good thing.

"Crying again?" Shinobu scoffed—but his tone was slightly different than before. "What you want to be, how you wanted to be born . . . I have no idea what you're talking about, but fine. You've disappointed your parents, as well?" he asked, oddly sympathetic as he let go of Karin's hand.

Karin was in no condition to wonder why. She just kept crying.

Shinobu sighed, glancing toward the street, but he suddenly stiffened. He pulled a tissue out of his pocket and shoved it at Karin. "Wipe your face!"

"Huh?"

"Quickly! And follow my lead! Don't you dare say anything!"

Karin was wiping her face with the tissue when she heard the squeal of brakes from the street. A car had stopped at the entrance to the alley. The woman behind the wheel leaned across the passenger seat, opened the window, and yelled, "I thought that was you, Shinobu! What are you doing here? I thought you were going to cram for school today? Is that a friend of yours?"

Karin had heard that slow, sweet drawl before. This was the woman who had dropped off Ayaha and Shinobu at school the previous morning. Shinobu glanced sincerely at Karin before walking toward the car. Karin followed him, frightened by what he would do to her otherwise.

"I thought that was your car, Mom," Shinobu said. "I saw you drive aimlessly the other way and make a U-turn."

Shinobu's mother frowned. "Aimlessly? How mean. I thought you might be in the area, so I was going slowly. It looks as though I was right! You're so beautiful, I could find you anywhere!"

"I still say that you should try to avoid boasting about your own child so brazenly. And no boy wants to be called beautiful."

"Aw, nobody minds if it's true. You agree, don't you?" Shinobu's mother said, glancing at Karin. "Oh my! Have you been crying?"

Before Karin could say anything, Shinobu lied, "Something got under her contact, and she finally managed to get it out."

"How awful! Is it all better now? If you'd like, I could give you a ride. It would give you a chance to clean your face. I'll drive you straight home! No girl wants to walk around with her face all red and puffy! You need to cool down. I have some wet tissues. Where do you live?"

"N-no, I have to go to work," Karin explained. The woman seemed so nice, but her son had ruthlessly threatened Karin moments ago, and she was still frightened.

"Oh my! Work? But you're only in high school!" the woman gasped.

Shinobu sighed. "Maaka's family encourages independence. They don't give her any allowance, and they expect her to buy her own necessities."

"How mature! If only Shinobu took after you. Maaka, was it? What's your first name?"

"K-Karin."

"Oh, what an adorable name! I just love girls. Did you know that, Karin? Shinobu begged his father for a motorcycle, and he drives around on it. Isn't that awful? Boys are always trying to do dangerous things. Once . . ." She seemed to be gearing up to talk forever.

Shinobu sighed again as he opened the back door. "Get in, Maaka. Mom, you know the family restaurant between here and cram school, right? That's where she works." Holding the door for Karin, he added in a low voice, "She'll talk until you get in." Taking the hint, Karin climbed in, sliding across to the other seat. Shinobu sat down next to her and closed the door.

"Are your contacts fixed? Shinobu, get those wet tissues. You need to cool off your eyes and nose, Karin," Shinobu's mother instructed happily as she drove away. "Are you Shinobu's girlfriend? You'll have to come by our house sometime. I'll bake a cake! Which do you like better, cheesecake or chocolate cake? If you'd like, you can help make it. I have an extra apron—a very cute one with frills. Aya likes eating cake, but she never helps bake them. Such a shame!"

Karin tensed at Ougimachi's name. *That's right— she lives in Kirioka's house* . . . As Karin wiped her face with the tissue, the strain in her face remained hidden from the rearview mirror.

Shinobu's mother chattered on. "I always wanted a girl! I wanted to wear matching clothes, bake cakes with her, and go shopping together. You can't do that with a boy!"

"I go shopping with you and carry your bags!" exclaimed Shinobu.

"I wanted to go out with a girl!"

"Sorry. Still male."

"When Shinobu was little, it was loads of fun. I'd put him and Aya in matching dresses and take them to the park. Everyone thought they were sisters! Hee hee hee. Shinobu's so beautiful—I'm sure he'd still look good. Don't you think so, Karin?"

"Um . . ." Karin had no idea how to respond. She glanced at Shinobu, but she was unable to tell from his expression if it was okay to laugh. There was no telling what he would do if she reacted the wrong way.

Shinobu's mother continued to babble: "Shinobu used to study ballet as Aya did, but he quit. He started going to the gym—or the *dojo*—I don't really know. It was some barbaric place like that, and now he's riding his motorbike around. I just hate how violent boys are. Shinobu's smart and beautiful, and a good boy—but I would much rather have had a girl."

Karin shivered, suddenly sensing a tiny wave of unhappiness from Shinobu. She stole a sideways glance at him, but he was smiling, listening to his mother. His gaze was turned toward the window, though, and Karin wasn't sure if that was a conscious choice or just coincidence. *So, this is what he meant by, "You've disappointed your parents, as well?" His mother might not be insulting him directly, but it must be pretty hard to hear . . .* His mother saying that she'd rather have a girl was essentially rejecting her son. Karin's own parents and brother had often called her a failure—or defective—but they'd never said that they would rather her be an ordinary vampire.

Karin could see Julian to the left. Shinobu leaned forward and interrupted his mother: "Mom, stop here. Maaka works at that restaurant. I'll get out here, too."

"Oh? I'll take you to cram school," she offered.

"It's only another block or two—and I have a few more things I want to talk with Maaka about."

"Ah. Karin, will you come over sometime soon? Shinobu never brings his friends home with him. It's so disappointing. I'd love to have a lot of girls visit. You will come, won't you?"

"Um, sure," Karin replied reluctantly.

Shinobu and Karin got out of the car, watching his mother drive away.

Hanging his head, Shinobu lamented, "I'm sorry you had to listen to that. Thank you for not saying anything."

"Is this what you meant by disappointing your parents? Has your mom always said she wanted a girl?" Karin asked, probing to find the root of unhappiness she'd sensed in the car.

With his eyes still fixed on the ground, Shinobu smiled ruefully and kicked a pebble. "Yeah, but everyone talks like that. 'If only we lived a little closer to the station . . .' or 'If only I had a different teacher." She doesn't mean anything more by it than that—she's merely grumbling about her life a bit. You could tell, right? She was born rich, and never lacked for anything." The pebble had bounced across the pavement into the planters between the sidewalk and the restaurant parking lot. "My mom loves me as much as other parents love their children, with the caveat that I have to be good. Another ten years, and I'll be my own man. I won't need my parents anymore. I can forget about them. That's much better than being a girl and serving as her dress-up doll my whole life."

Karin could no longer detect any unhappiness, proving that this wasn't only sour grapes. Shinobu seemed to be able to control his own way of thinking. But the wounds probably opened whenever his mother repeated those words.

There was no way Shinobu could have known what Karin was thinking, but he turned and peered directly at her. "And to be clear, the fact that I wore a skirt when I was younger doesn't give you any advantage over me. It was never what I wanted—only what my mother insisted upon. Tell anyone you want."

"I-I would never!" Karin exclaimed.

"Thanks. Back to Aya . . ."

Karin shivered.

They were no longer in a back alley, but on a busy street. A lot of cars were driving past, and the pair were in sight of restaurant windows. Shinobu obviously didn't intend to take any more drastic measures.

"You're sure she'll be back to normal in a month? With no lingering effects?" Shinobu asked.

"Y-yes, I'm sure. Really . . ." Karin was still frightened, and her fear was evident in her voice.

Shinobu nodded. "Fine. I'd still like to know what you actually did, but I'll let you off the hook, because you put up with my mother and didn't tell her anything. I'm choosing to trust your word. Bye." He waved and walked away.

Karin watched him leave, rubbing her thumb. It still hurt a little. When Shinobu had threatened her in the alley, he'd seemed so violent and frightening— nothing like a straight-A student. But when she met his mother, she'd realized that she and Shinobu shared a similar pain. Because of that, his words weighed particularly heavily upon her.

Shinobu had said, "Changing someone's personality against her will is unforgivable!" Karin hadn't meant to. The only way for her to live safely as a reverse vampire was to bite people and inject her blood into them. The personality change was only a side effect—and there was nothing she could do about it. The same side effect occurred when her parents and brother drank blood. As the blood left their bodies, so did their stress and their desire to lie.

Karin was drawn toward unhappy people, and she gave them mental strength as she injected them. She did feel bad about abruptly attacking and biting them, but she comforted herself with the fact that it ultimately made them feel better. The change in their personalities had made her feel *less* guilty about biting them, until now. *What should I do?* She really wanted to see Kenta. He would know the answer.

Even though Kenta had learned what Karin was, he'd insisted that no one—humans or vampires—deserved to have their place stolen. If only she could see his face and hear his voice. She almost took her phone out of her bag before remembering Kenta didn't have a cell phone. Karin had a home phone number, but he wouldn't be home yet. *He went to investigate the development plan today. . . .* By now, they must've reached Ayaha's house, and they were probably eating some kind of snack. Karin could feel her chest tightening as she imagined it. *Kenta . . . I want to see you!*

Still standing on the sidewalk, Karin hung her head.

A voice called out from the parking lot: "Maaka, is something wrong?" It was Kobayashi, who worked at Julian with her; she was taking out the trash. "What are you doing standing there? Do you feel sick?"

"N-no, I'm fine. I'd better change!"

Everyone else was working hard. Karin wiped her eyes and ran toward the staff entrance.

Kenta was outside the gates of the Ougimachi home, getting out of a taxi after Ayaha, who paid with a taxi ticket.

"Are you normally driven to school?" asked Kenta.

"No, I took the bus when I lived here. But the bus stop is so far from the house that I had to walk fifteen minutes! And there were so few buses—so my dad gave me these tickets to use when I couldn't be bothered."

Kenta could feel the difference in their economic situations being pounded into him. He sighed. He would walk fifteen or thirty minutes; and if there were only one bus per hour, he would still wait.

"Shino's house is much closer to school and the ballet studio. I was supposed to go to a private high school called Saint Anna Maria, but I got sick and was in the hospital while the tests were held—so I ended up at First High," explained Ayaha.

"Oh . . ."

"But I'm glad. Anna Maria is a girls' school, so I never would have seen Shino, and I never would have been able to make friends with you." She flashed a smile at Kenta, who nodded weakly back.

Mmm . . . she's not a bad person, but I can't get past the arrogant impression she gave off at first, Kenta thought to himself. Ayaha was easy to get along with now, but that was temporary, and it was only the case because Karin had bit her. *It was because her personality changed that we found out about the development plan—but now I feel like I'm taking advantage of her. She brought the subject up, though, and we're in too much trouble to worry about that.*

While Kenta was thinking, Ayaha pushed the intercom button and spoke into the mouthpiece. Eventually, an old woman in a short-sleeved dress and apron opened the gate from the inside. "Welcome home, miss."

"Nice to be back, Toki. Sorry for leaving Dad and the house up to you all this time. But because you were here, I know they were in good hands," Ayaha said, smiling.

The housekeeper blinked at Ayaha in disbelief. "Miss, did something good happen to you?"

"Why?"

"Well, you seem to be in very good spirits."

Kenta knew exactly how the housekeeper felt. Ayaha had become a great deal more personable, which must have come as quite a surprise to someone who hadn't seen her in a while.

As Ayaha was unaware of any difference, she simply laughed. "Don't say that! It sounds like I'm usually in a bad mood. Ah, this is my friend Usui. Dad's still at work, right? What time's he getting home?"

"These days, he never gets home before midnight."

"Oh. Oh, well. To be honest, I'm not really home to stay. I only came to pick up some warmer clothes, and then I'm right back to Auntie's house. As long as that woman is here, I'm not."

The housekeeper seemed disappointed. "Oh . . . if you don't move back in, Michiko will only get more and more heavy-handed. She's already acting as if she's always lived here, changing the décor and whatnot!"

Ayaha scowled. "Did she touch my mother's room?"

"No, only the reception room and guest bedrooms. Personally, I consider that more than enough, but I am merely a humble servant. If the master approved of it, there's nothing I can do."

"Is she here?"

"She left two hours ago. She said she was going to the beauty salon, but who knows where she really is."

Ayaha bit her lip. "Stupid Daddy," she muttered. But then, she shook her head as if changing her mind. "We're here to get clothes today. Usui came to help me carry them. I don't need dinner, but if we could get some tea?"

"Certainly, certainly. I do apologize for bringing up such unpleasantness. We old ladies do love to grumble!"

"Not at all. Usui knows what's going on. Otherwise, I'd never bring him here. Come on in."

"Um . . . thanks." Kenta went through the gate, and once inside, cocked his head as he observed the house. It was surrounded by high concrete walls, so he hadn't been able to see it from the outside. It was a modern house of concrete and iron framework, with block glass—and he'd seen it somewhere before.

Ayaha walked straight across the paving stones through the garden and opened the front door. "Dad's study is on the second floor. This way." She had come home to get winter clothes, but as she led Kenta to the study, it became apparent that she wanted to take care of his business first.

Despite the fact that the man's daughter was leading him, Kenta was reluctant to step inside Ayaha's father's room. "Are you sure? I mean, it wasn't locked, but still . . ." Kenta said, stopping in the doorway and looking around the room that smelled of tobacco.

Ayaha immediately walked toward the massive desk and began opening files. "It's fine. I'm pretty sure it was called Nishi-ku Akamagaoka Royal Executive Platinum Estates. It was in a blue binder on the desk when I saw it. Dad's a little careless with his things—

including documents. Hmm . . . it isn't here. Maybe he took it to work with him."

That was likely. Kenta scratched his head. "Well, if it isn't here . . ."

"Usui, you need to know what's in it, right?"

"But the documents aren't here, so—"

"Yeah, but maybe he left a copy. Finding it would be a pain, though," Ayaha concluded, sighing at a rack jammed full of papers. Suddenly, a thought crossed her mind and she brightened up. "Of course! I'll call Dad this evening and ask! What did you want to know?"

"Um . . . when construction starts, when they plan to start talking to people about moving or eviction, and the exact location."

"They might already be evicting people. I think he said he was trying to get final approval from city hall. You can't do that if you aren't sure you can secure the land."

"Oh . . ." Kenta grew sullen. He had guessed as much, but the plan already had involved so many people. This was well beyond the stage where the Maaka vampires could erase people's memories and stop the development. *I'll have to call Karin later . . . but I don't have any good news for her.*

All of a sudden, the sound of slippers could be heard traipsing down the hall. As Ayaha guessed to whom the footsteps belonged, her mood quickly soured. Kenta stared at the open door nervously.

Standing in the doorway was a woman in a kimono, her hair pulled up. If you roughly divided all women's faces into two types—*kitsune* and *tanuki*—this one would, without a doubt, be the former. Her eyes were pulled back at the edges, and she reeked of confidence, which alarmed Kenta. There also was an allure in her eyes as she glanced around the room that spoke to his baser instincts. He could see how men would fall for her. "Welcome home, Ayaha."

Ayaha didn't respond, and instead flipped through the file before putting it away. It was only at that point that she glanced at the door. "Oh, were you visiting, Mitsuyo?"

"Michiko. And I happen to live here. Or did you sniff glue or take some other drug that damaged your memories before gracing us with your presence?"

"It's pretty hard for the average high school student to obtain drugs of that sort—unlike some people I could name, who worked as a hostess in a shop of ill repute. I'm sorry to have gotten your name wrong, but I can't be bothered to remember the names of all my father's mistresses."

Kenta shivered. Each of the women was maintaining a perfectly polite tone and expression, but there were invisible fireworks exploding between them. Merely listening to them was enough to give him an ulcer.

Michiko's eyes flashed angrily, and a faint smile crept onto the corners of her lips. "I can see how you'd forget what's happening at home, given how you abandoned your father in favor of sleeping wherever strikes your fancy. And the fact that you're his daughter doesn't give you the right to walk into his study and rifle through his belongings, especially when you've brought a strange boy with you."

Kenta stiffened, but Ayaha raised her voice, defending him. "No need for you to concern yourself with such matters, Michiko. This boy is my friend, and father is more than pleased when I show interest in his work. He told me he plans to hand over control of the company to me and my husband someday. Being his daughter grants me privileges a mere mistress could never dream of."

Michiko raised her eyebrow. It was an expression that jogged Kenta's memory. "Oh! I remember now!" he yelped. Her hairstyle had been different the last time they'd met, but Kenta recognized her now.

"What is it, Usui?" Ayaha asked.

"I thought I'd seen this house before, and now I know why. I worked for a delivery company this summer, and I helped deliver to this house, right?" he asked, looking to Michiko for confirmation.

Michiko gasped, flustered, which struck Kenta as odd.

"Usui, the air in here has turned foul and reeks of heavy makeup. We shall take our tea elsewhere. I'm sure Toki has it ready." Ayaha took Kenta's arm, pulling him into the hall, so he never had a chance to hear Michiko's response.

Ah well—it doesn't really matter if I've been here before. Or so Kenta thought. If he'd seen Michiko's expression, he quickly would've changed his mind.

As she listened to the kids' footsteps go down the stairs, Michiko took her cell phone out of her purse, unable to hide the impatience and anxiety on her face. "Hello, Ryuji? It's me, Michiko. You kept the battery charged, for once. No, there's something I need to talk about. Wait for me in the usual spot." He seemed reluctant, so her voice sharpened. "This isn't a joke! One false move, and I'll be out on the street. Then, I won't be able to pay your allowance. See? I'll be there as soon as I can."

When Michiko hung up, she glared spitefully at the spot where Kenta had been standing. "Little bitch has some dangerous friends . . . but how?"

About an hour later, Michiko was in a dimly lit café. It was a café in name only—there was nothing fancy about the coffee or cake served there. Each seat was partitioned off into a kind of private little room, as if a major part of the establishment's business came from people wishing to meet in secret.

Sitting across from Michiko was a young man with a mustache. His shirt was open and gold chains glittered across his chest.

"I'm sure of it," Michiko said. "Near the end of August, when I called the antique shop, that boy came to deliver." She shivered. Michiko had kept her gambling habit secret from her patron, Katsuaki Ougimachi. When she'd lost big and was desperate for money, she'd sold two or three things from the house to an antique shop. A friend had introduced her to an antiques dealer, and she had called him to the house while Katsuaki was at work and the housekeeper was out shopping.

By chance, a package had been delivered the same day. Without thinking about it, Michiko had let the delivery boy in and took the package. "He was the high school boy Ayaha brought home with her today. He heard me talking about antiques, and he saw me hand over the vase and censer. If he thinks about it, he'll realize I was selling them!"

Postmen, caterers, and delivery boys—they all might as well be invisible. Nobody remembered them as individuals, which is why Michiko thought nothing of letting Kenta in. But the person she'd assumed she would never see again had turned out to be Ayaha's friend.

Michiko was clearly irritated and panicky, but the man only shrugged. "I think you're overreacting."

"I don't," Michiko insisted. "The boy even asked to make sure it was me, and he said that he remembered going there. I'm sure of it, Ryuji. He was threatening me! I'm sure he was thinking, 'I know you sold things from this house to the antique dealers.' Twisting the screws. He had evil eyes—like no ordinary high school boy."

"And your patron hasn't noticed that you sold them?"

"He's been so busy at work that he falls asleep the moment he gets home. We never use the guest room, so how would he notice anything missing from it? I changed the décor, so the housekeeper didn't notice, either. But if they go looking for something missing, I'm sure they'll notice." Michiko lit a cigarette. She took a long drag off it, but it seemed to make her more impatient. "The daughter has always hated me. If the delivery boy suggests that something is missing, she'll have a great time ransacking the house, finding proof, and kicking me to the curb."

"Can't you use your appeal to keep the father on your side?"

"Impossible, impossible. Katsuaki isn't that naive. He won't let me marry him as long as his daughter refuses to accept it, and he still only gives me my regular allowance. He won't let me control his money. If he found out I'd sold something from the house, he'd kick me out without another penny.

Ugh! What should I do? Ryuji, can you think of anything?"

"That's what you get for gambling. You're an amateur," Michiko's brother grinned.

"Do you intend to help me or not?" Michiko snapped.

Ryuji didn't seem embarrassed. He swiped a cigarette from Michiko's cigarette case and lit it. "Of course. I always do. I do have an idea—but it might mean getting a little rough."

Michiko waited for the rest of her brother's brilliant idea.

"This delivery boy and the master's daughter are an item, yeah? He might already have told her what you did, which means we have to silence them both before they have a chance to tell Katsuaki."

"Ryuji . . . you mean . . ." Michiko nearly dropped her cigarette.

Ryuji leaned across the table, lowering his voice. "High school kids these days are so unstable. You never know when they'll up and kill themselves. Last week, two high school girls jumped off the roof of their school holding hands. I simply have to make it look like that—Ayaha and this boy jumping to their deaths holding hands . . . no one will suspect a thing."

"Maybe so, but—"

"Think about it. The only reason Katsuaki won't marry you is because his daughter is against it. If his daughter dies, all you have to do is comfort him in his grief. He'd be so happy that he'd be glad to marry you. And then, you'll get the whole fortune. Two birds with one stone, so to speak."

Michiko was speechless.

"We don't have time for you to think it over. If Katsuaki finds out, we're done for, right?"

"I . . . I . . ." Michiko hesitated. She hated Ayaha Ougimachi. The girl always mocked her. She was an arrogant, spoiled, selfish child. Michiko would like nothing more than to grab Ayaha's cheeks and twist them—but she'd never wanted to kill her. Murder was a much more serious crime than theft or a con job. What should she do to keep herself safe? Still unsure Michiko shook her head. "I . . . could never do it. Everyone knows Ayaha and I don't get along. If she died, they'd suspect me."

"Nah, nah, don't worry. I'll take care of it. Anything for you."

"Y-you don't mind?"

"You're my sister. Leave it to me. Taking out a couple of kids is nothing. So, the daughter and this kid are still in the Ougimachi house? Are they spending the night?" Ryuji didn't even hesitate, which made him seem a little frivolous—but Michiko didn't have anyone else who could help her.

Still wavering, Michiko replied, "The housekeeper wasn't making dinner, so I doubt it. They didn't seem as though they were staying long. When I left the house, they were eating cake, but—"

"Go home quickly, and try to keep them there. I'll wait for them to leave, yank them into a car, and take them somewhere. You stay in the house and wait to hear that she's dead. Oh, do you have any cash on you? I have a loan I need to pay back today. Fifty thousand should cover it." Ryuji flashed his sister a sleazy grin.

Michiko bit her lip. Her brother's idea was so simple and direct that it worried her. Would it really be that easy? If Kenta had told Ayaha about her—and if Katsuaki found out, and kicked Michiko out—all this time she'd spent enjoying the privileges of being his mistress would have been wasted. She had no time to plan carefully. The only way to protect her position was to take both of them out before news reached Katsuaki's ears.

The scales in Michiko's heart began to tip. "Okay. If they've already left, I'll call you again. The girl will go to her aunt Kirioka's house—and if you ask the delivery company, you can probably get them to give you the boy's address." Michiko opened her wallet, took out all the money, and gave it to her brother. "If you're going to do this, you'd better be sure they can't talk. The daughter . . . and the delivery boy."

CHIBI VAMPIRE AND KENTA IN PERIL

Karin's phone rang faintly inside the locker. She had her uniform half off, but she stopped undressing. She was alone in the locker room, and she could talk half undressed. Quickly pulling out the phone, Karin saw that the screen read: "Kenta Usui." Her blood stopped flowing. A moment later, it started rushing again at twice the speed. Her eyes felt hot. *Kenta!*

Kenta didn't have a cell phone, so Karin always had to wait for him to call her. "Hello, this is Karin! Kenta?"

"Y-yeah, this is Kenta. Is something wrong?" Kenta asked sounding surprised.

Karin must have been a little too excited—so much so that she nearly burst into tears. It had been almost four hours since she'd parted company with Shinobu. At the cost of a little pain, she'd managed to confirm that her identity wasn't suspected. Shinobu was a die-hard realist and refused to consider the notion of vampires at all—luckily. But Shinobu's harshest words, "Changing someone's personality against her will is unforgivable," remained buried deep in her heart and had begun to twist around.

Karin had been too busy at work to think about it much, but the moment she heard Kenta's voice, all the tension flooded out of her. "Kenta . . . um . . . um . . ." The feelings were churning around inside her, and she could barely talk.

Kenta asked, puzzled, "What's wrong, Karin? Where are you—still at work? I could call back."

"No, I'm finished with work! Kenta, do you mind if I come over now?" she hurriedly cried, afraid he would hang up.

"Come over . . . to my place?"

Going to a boy's house this late at night *was* a little bold.

"Um, I didn't mean it like that. I wanted to hear about today, that's all."

"Well, the documents weren't in Ougimachi's dad's study, so we still don't have any details. He must have taken them to work—and the housekeeper says he's always home really late. Ougimachi promised to call him and get the information later."

"O-oh . . ."

"Yeah. But I'm going to go by the Ougimachi house again now. Maybe Ougimachi's dad will be home and I can ask about the plan."

"Again? You already went . . ."

"Yeah, but someone called from there, saying they wanted to give me something to thank me for helping out today. They said it wouldn't keep until tomorrow. I guess it must be food."

It seemed awfully backward to summon someone to thank him after he'd arrived home, but Kenta didn't seem to mind.

"It sounded as though there was more to it than that—and it's not like I'm doing anything else. My mother's busy working tonight," explained Kenta.

"Oh, good. She found a job?" asked Karin.

"No, just a one-day thing cleaning up after some concert. But she's happy to get anything she can—even a one-off job like this. So, anyway, I'll call you again when I get back from Ougimachi's. Bye."

After Kenta hung up, Karin stood there clutching her phone in silence. She eventually recovered and finished changing, but she remained hopelessly depressed. *Kenta's going to see Ougimachi again. Amemiya-shi is to the east? He'll have to take a bus there, and they're making him come all the way back . . . ?*

Perhaps the idea of a thank-you that involved food had tempted Kenta. He was forever hungry, so that was possible—but maybe he was secretly looking forward to seeing Ayaha again. *Kenta, I want to see you. I'm so worried. I don't know what to do.* Karin wanted to hear Kenta's voice—see his face. No matter how scared she was, if she saw him, it all would fade to nothing and her body would fill with warmth. Merely a glimpse would be enough.

Karin left Julian. There wasn't a moon in the darkened sky above. The stars were glittering faintly, but they only made her feel lonely. "Ah . . . no . . ." She stopped, troubled by a pebble in her shoe. She was right by the bus stop. There was nobody on the bench, which was bathed in a pool of light. After she sat down, she took off her shoe, got the pebble out, and put her shoe back on.

As Karin stood up, a bus slowed down and stopped in front of her. The driver must have mistaken her for a passenger, because he opened the door. "No, I . . ." Karin started to shake her head, but then she froze when she noticed that the sign on the bus read, "Amemiya-shi Council Chambers." *Kenta said Ougimachi's house is very close to that.* The thought that Kenta must be going that way gave her feet wings. She could think of nothing else as she drifted onto the bus.

Forty minutes later, Karin was standing in the evening wind in front of the Ougimachi residence, clutching her cheeks in embarrassment. *Wh-why did I come here?*

Some sort of fever had driven Karin onto the bus, and when she'd stepped off it, she'd ended up directly across from a police box. Her eyes had met those of a friendly looking policeman on the other side of the glass, and when he'd smiled at her, she'd found herself walking in and asking for directions to Ougimachi's house. It had taken twenty minutes to walk to the house, but the directions were easy to follow—so she arrived safely. More important, she'd finally come to her senses by the time she arrived.

Karin hardly could push the intercom button. She had no reason to be at Ougimachi's house, so she couldn't hang around the gate like some sort of stalker. She was clueless as to whether Kenta had reached the house, was still there, or had already gone home. Really—what was she doing? All she could think was that anxiety and loneliness had driven her mad. *Yikes! If Kenta came out now and ran into me, how would I explain what I'm doing? It's so embarrassing—like I was waiting to ambush him!*

No sooner had Karin become overwhelmed by all these realizations than she heard a sound from behind the tall walls. She quickly hid in the shadow of the pillar attached to the house across the street. The pillar was next to the gate, but it wasn't the front gate that opened. The automatic shutter on the garage next to it did, sliding upward with a low rumble. A car slowly slid out. The driver was an unfamiliar thuggish-looking man with a mustache. Someone appeared to be sitting in the passenger seat, too, but Karin couldn't work out who it was from her vantage point.

The car pulled out onto the road and stopped. A woman in a kimono walked out of the garage and spoke to the driver. There was nothing around but big houses, so it was quiet enough for Karin to hear the conversation. "Are you sure this is okay, Ryuji? Everything's gone wrong. I'm sure the housekeeper must think it strange that I suddenly sent her out on an errand."

"It'll be fine, sis. Both the daughter and the delivery boy bought the fake phone call, right? You're worrying about nothing. Get back inside."

The man's words made Karin's nerves tingle. Kenta had worked as a delivery boy during the summer. Did the man mean him? The way the man and the woman were both keeping an eye on their surroundings was suspicious. Karin remained hidden in the shadows, listening very intently.

The woman went back inside the garage. As the shutter closed, the man called through it, "Don't worry! They're both sound asleep. All I have to do is push them over the edge! High school students love to follow trends. Everyone will believe they decided to copy the lovers' suicide from earlier this summer."

Push them over the edge? What's he talking about? Karin's body temperature was plummeting, but her heart was beating very quickly. The car began driving again, passing in front of Karin's hiding place. *Kenta!* She caught a clear glimpse of Kenta in the passenger seat, slumped over, with his head resting against the glass. His posture was unnatural, his eyes were closed, and he wasn't moving. Had he been drugged?

"Kenta!" Karin jumped out into the street, calling her friend's name—but as the car sped away, the sound of the engine drowned out her voice. She ran after it, but the car was too fast. Its taillights were out of sight in a matter of moments.

Karin slowed to a stop, out of breath. *What's he going to do to Kenta?* This wasn't good at all. She was so worried about Kenta that she was trembling. But there was no way she could keep up with a moving car. She remembered the kimono woman in the house. *That woman must know where he's taking Kenta . . .* Karin spun around and ran back toward the Ougimachi home.

Suddenly, a roar came up behind her. She thought it was the car coming back, but it was a motorcycle. As Karin moved to the side of the road, the motorcycle raced past her, pulling up in front of the Ougimachi garage. The driver, wearing a black denim shirt and jeans, got off and looked at Karin. "Maaka, why are you here?"

When Karin saw Shinobu Kirioka's face scowling suspiciously at her through the screen of the helmet, Karin's entire body grew hot. She had heard that Shinobu had done something to drive away all the boys that lurked around Ayaha. He also had threatened to break Karin's finger, so he obviously didn't hesitate to get violent. And now Kenta, who Ayaha had asked out, had been summoned by a fake phone call and was driven away somewhere. For Shinobu to show up now meant he must have something to do with it.

As Karin mulled over the possibilities in her head, her body shook, the cork popped out, and a deluge of tears and screaming gushed out of her. "Uuuuuugh, you idiot!"

"What?" Shinobu asked flippantly.

"Stupid, stupid, stupid, stupid Kirioka! You big meanie!" Karin wailed, with no sense of shame at all. She grabbed Shinobu. "What did Kenta ever do? He never did anything! Where did you take him? What are you going to do to him?"

"Your nose is running."

"To hell with that! And what did they mean by lovers' suicide? Are you going to kill Kenta?"

Shinobu's eyes narrowed. "Lovers' suicide?"

"Yes! I heard the guy driving the car talking to the woman in the kimono! You know who they are, don't you? Because Ougimachi asked Kenta out, you're going to get him out of the picture . . . you big meanie! Please, call them, and make them stop! Make them stop!"

"You can't carry out a lovers' suicide alone," Shinobu muttered, sounding genuinely puzzled. He frowned, thinking hard.

"K-Kirioka . . . you don't know?"

"You said someone was driving, and that person took Usui with him? From Aya's . . . from the Ougimachi house?"

"Yes. You really didn't tell him to do it? Kenta was asleep in the front seat, I think. A man with a mustache drove him away."

"If I'd planned it, I never would have hired people dumb enough to talk about it where you could overhear them." The coldness in Shinobu's voice was very convincing. Apparently, he really didn't have anything to do with it.

"Then, what? Is Kenta . . . ?" The lingering questions made Karin shiver more severely. Someone else had taken Kenta away. But where?

"How long ago was this?"

"Only a few minutes ago. When I heard your bike, I thought it was the car coming back."

Shinobu glanced in the direction he'd come, but the car was long gone, and there was no way to tell where it had gone. "You mentioned a woman in a kimono. Did she have narrow eyes and heavy makeup—like a hostess?"

Karin nodded.

"Did she get into the car?" Shinobu asked.

"No, she went back into the house. The mustache guy called her his sister. What are they going to do to Kenta?"

Because Shinobu was able to describe the woman, it was clear that he knew who the man and woman were—and he might be able to guess why Kenta had been dragged away. Shinobu took off his helmet, repeating what he'd said a moment before. "You can't have a lovers' suicide alone. Usui is only a partner . . . *probably* only a partner."

"What do you mean?" Karin shrieked, not catching Shinobu's drift.

"Aya hasn't come home yet—not to my home, anyway. She and Usui came back once around five, but then Usui called her, and she went out again."

"That's weird! Kenta called me earlier and said Ougimachi had called him and asked him to come back here!"

"Both calls were fake. At any rate, about a half an hour after Aya left, my mother remembered something and called Aya's cell phone—but the call didn't go through. My mother got worried and began to panic. She said that a boy had called Aya out after dark and that she wasn't answering her phone, so something must have happened. Then, she sent me out to look for her." Shinobu glanced down at his bike. "I went to Usui's house, but the lights were off, and no one was home. I searched everywhere else I could think of before coming here. When I saw you here, I wondered if you were partly responsible for calling Aya out, but—"

"I didn't!"

"Yeah. I'd put the nail in that pretty well. And I'd be really impressed if you could cry and run at the nose like that to hide your involvement."

Karin's lips did taste of salt. Her tears were one thing, but if she had snot running down her face, that was horrible. Karin quickly turned her back on Shinobu. She rummaged around in her bag, looking for tissues, and wiped her tears and blew her nose.

"So, why are you here?" Shinobu inquired.

"Uh, um . . ." Karin stared at the ground. She'd wanted to see Kenta so much that she'd drifted onto a bus and arrived at Ayaha's before she knew it—but that was far too embarrassing to admit.

"It's not important. I'm much more concerned with Aya's whereabouts. She's probably not here, but it's worth asking." Shinobu went to the gate and pressed the intercom button.

A sexy woman's voice answered: "Who is it?"

"Shinobu Kirioka. Michiko? Is Aya there?"

"Ayaha? She went home ages ago. Did you come to pick her up?"

Shinobu's eyebrows lifted slightly, but his voice remained perfectly calm. "Guess I must have missed her. I wasn't coming to meet her, though. My mother sent me to bring something to my uncle. It's some kind of disc. Do you mind if I leave it with you?"

"Certainly. Just a minute," answered the woman.

As the intercom cut out, Shinobu scowled. "If Michiko answered herself, Toki must be out. That's not a good sign. Maaka?"

"Hmm? Wh-what?" Karin asked, nervously.

"You should go home," Shinobu urged in a grave tone. "This isn't going to be a fun conversation to watch. Frankly, you'll only get in my way."

"What do you mean?"

"The woman you heard just now was Michiko, Aya's father's mistress. She's hoping to be elevated to wife now that his wife is dead; unfortunately, her lover's daughter absolutely refuses to permit it. In other words, Aya is getting in Michiko's way. Usui was driven away in a car by Michiko's brother, Aya's missing, and you heard them mention a lovers' suicide. Do I need to connect the dots?"

Karin gulped.

"Was Aya in the car?" Shinobu asked.

"I don't know . . . I only saw Kenta."

"She might have been lying on the backseat. You'd better go home. I'll take care of the rest."

"N-no! Kenta might be—" Karin yelped, but her ability to emit sound was cut off from the inside.

Michiko left the house and the gate opened. "Hello, Shinobu. I'll take that disc."

It was definitely the woman who had seen the car off. As Karin began backing away, she cringed at the insectoid tinge to the woman's phony smile.

"Mm? What?" asked Shinobu.

Michiko frowned at Karin. As Karin was about to yell at the mistress and ask what she'd done with Kenta, Shinobu grabbed her arm and pulled it hard, causing an electric shock to race all the way down to Karin's fingers. Shinobu exclaimed merrily, "See? I told you! She looks exactly like Anastasia Eliskaya!"

Karin didn't know what Shinobu meant, but the pain in her elbow was too unbearable for her to say anything. Realizing that he wanted her to follow his lead, she nodded.

Shinobu glanced back at Michiko, grinning. "Sorry! This is my girlfriend, and she was visiting my house today. She's a big theatre fan—and when I told her you look exactly like the Russian actress Anastasia, she said that no Japanese person could ever have such a strong, beautiful nose. I had to prove it to her."

"Well, I'm honored to resemble an actress," replied Michiko.

"Because I had to deliver the disc anyway, I brought her along. Mm? What?" Shinobu bent down, pretending to listen, although Karin hadn't said anything. Then, he muttered, "Yeah, yeah," and turned back toward Michiko. "Sorry . . . can she use your bathroom?"

Few people could turn down such a request from someone they knew. Michiko beckoned them through the gate.

As the pair followed Michiko inside, Karin whispered, "Does she really look like a Russian actress?"

"God, no! You seemed scared when you saw her, so I made up an actress to compare her to," explained Shinobu. It was quite a lie to come up with on the spot. "And you got us inside. Once we're in, I can ask anything I want. And because no one came out when you were screaming and crying, we don't have to worry about noise."

"Noise? Kirioka!" What was Shinobu going to do? He'd only pretended he was going to break Karin's finger, but was he really going to do it this time? Fear had made Karin's voice a little too loud.

Michiko glanced back at Shinobu and Karin, who kept her gaze down, refusing to meet Michiko's eye. "What are you whispering about?"

"Nothing. I mentioned that I'm much more of a bad boy than I look, and hinted at what we're going to do next," replied Shinobu.

"My, my—were you?" Michiko smirked, obviously enjoying what she'd read into Shinobu's words. "But you seem so well behaved—like a straight-A student. My man bragged about what a great nephew he had. Surprising."

"You can have good grades and still behave badly. Shall I prove it to you?"

"Sure you want to say that in front of your girlfriend?" Michiko smirked, clearly treating Shinobu like a child who was talking big.

Once inside the house, Shinobu pointed to the back of the entrance hall. "Turn at the end of the hall, and the little door on the right is the bathroom. Go on. Michiko, could I trouble you for a cup of tea? I'm really thirsty."

"Sure. This way."

Obediently, Karin went off toward the toilet. She hadn't realized that she needed to use the bathroom, but as soon as she was in there, she felt as though she did. When she was finished, she came back to the entrance, but Shinobu and Michiko weren't there. *Where did they go?* Karin was too worried about Kenta to go home, but she felt uncomfortable walking around the house and opening doors at random. Being alone in a strange house made her feel as if she were some sort of burglar. She wandered down the hall aimlessly until she heard Michiko scream.

"Stop! Please, stop! Are you insane?" Michiko squealed.

Karin couldn't hear Shinobu's answer. Running toward the screams, she found the door and tried the knob, but it was locked from the inside. She shook the door, screaming, "Kirioka? Kirioka, what are you doing?"

"Hear that voice, Michiko? She saw your brother driving away with Usui and Aya in his car. There's no use pretending. Tell me where he took them," Shinobu insisted.

Karin heard a splashing sound and Michiko scream again.

"Stop it! If you do that, you'll be in trouble, too!" the mistress bellowed.

"Thanks for your concern. Don't worry—I'm a minor, and this is my first offense. If I pretend to feel remorse, I'll get off with a warning. What about you? Do you want to test how well plastic surgeons can cover scars?"

"S-stop . . ."

"That's not the word I want to hear. I warned you that I'm not nearly as well behaved as I look. It seems that you thought I meant something else, but you were wrong. I meant that I never hesitate to resort to violence. Like this."

"Stop! The school! Sugihashi . . . the abandoned elementary school! It's the same place those two girls jumped off the roof last month!"

"And that's the truth?"

"It is! Believe me!"

"Okay. If you're lying, I'll have to come back here, and we'll have to do this again. And next time, I'll use the burner."

Karin heard another shriek. The door was closed, and she couldn't see inside, so she didn't know exactly what was happening. Not knowing was more frightening than knowing, but she couldn't work up the nerve to knock and yell. Instead, she stood in the hall covering her mouth with her hands. All of a sudden, the door opened. "Eek!" Karin leapt back against the wall.

It was Shinobu. "Michiko can't reach her brother's phone. He always forgets to recharge it, apparently. She tried to call before I got here, to see how things were going. We have to head straight for the school."

"The s-school? He took Kenta there?" Karin asked.

It seemed like a strange place for a crime.

"With the declining birth rate, elementary schools get closed a lot—even in the city. Did you hear about the two high school girls who jumped off the roof holding hands earlier this summer? It was all over the news. Nobody goes there anymore, and there are rumors that the place is haunted. It's the perfect place to fake a lovers' suicide." As he spoke, Shinobu quickly walked down the hall toward the door.

Karin considered peeking into the room, but ended up following Shinobu instead. She was worried about Kenta. "Um, Kirioka . . . did you do anything to Michiko?"

"Nope. Didn't hurt her at all."

"No way! But she was screaming!"

"I didn't hurt her. I merely tied her up with plastic wrap and cut her hair with kitchen scissors—and because she still wouldn't say anything, I splashed salad oil in her face and lit the gas stove. As soon as I pretended I was going to push her face into the stove, she talked."

Shinobu detailed the events so casually that Karin gasped. Michiko may not have been physically injured, but she had undoubtedly gone through terrible mental trauma.

As Shinobu put his sneakers on, he announced, "I'll go to the school. You go home. If I have time, I'll call you and fill you in."

"B-but . . . !"

Shinobu obviously wasn't going to listen to Karin. His attention already was focused on the school. He went through the gate, put his helmet on, and climbed onto his motorcycle.

Karin chased after him, grabbing the mirror so he couldn't leave her. "Take me with you!" she screamed. "Kenta's in danger! I can't wait around at home! I'm coming, too!"

"If you do come, will you be able to help? You were terrified listening to what I did in there."

Karin had no answer for Shinobu's very true observation. There was nothing she could do. She might be a vampire, but she was defective—a blood-injector. She was very clumsy and couldn't erase memories. She was worse than most humans. Kenta always ended up saving her. Even so . . . "Please, take me! I'm so worried about Kenta. Please!" Tears rolled down her cheeks. She didn't want to lose Kenta, and she didn't want to think that Kenta might vanish from her life. "Please, take me to Kenta," she sniffled, still clutching the mirror.

Shinobu sighed. "You sure do cry a lot. I don't have time to talk you out of it. Don't get snot on my shirt, okay?"

"Ah! Thank you!"

"I have only one helmet, and I barely obtained my license two months ago—so I'm really not supposed to have a passenger. No, wipe your snot before you get on!"

"S-sorry . . . but if you can't have passengers, what were you going to do with Ougimachi?"

"Use my phone and call a taxi. Hold on tight. I'm going fast. If you fall off, I'm not coming back for you."

"O-oka . . . aaahhh! Wait! Too fast, too fast, too fast! Scaaary!"

"Don't talk. You'll bite your tongue!"

"Owww!"

There were no lights at all in the abandoned elementary school. There was a lake next to the building and a factory on the other side. The tax offices were across the street, so by eight o'clock, the area was completely silent and incredibly deserted.

The motorcycle carrying Shinobu and Karin went through the open gates, skidded across the yard, and stopped by the side of the school.

Shinobu jumped off the bike, took his helmet off, and glanced at the car parked nearby. "Is that Michiko's brother's car? Ryuji, was it? He must still be inside."

He didn't wait for Karin to answer. She'd managed to get off the bike by herself, but her body felt as though it was still swaying, and her knees were knocking together.

"Good thing we didn't crash. I've never driven sixty miles per hour on ordinary roads before, especially with a passenger," Shinobu declared calmly, taking off his jacket and hanging it on his bike handles.

When Shinobu began walking toward the school, Karin desperately forced her wobbly legs to follow him. The darkness was scary enough—but for the last few months, people had been talking about the ghosts of the two girls who'd killed themselves here. She was afraid to be left on her own—and she had to find Kenta. "I-I didn't know you were a speed demon, Kirioka. Y-you don't look like the motorcycle type."

Shinobu glanced back at Karin. "I was going fast because we were in a hurry, and I'm not a huge fan of motorcycles. Last spring, I happened to catch my father having an affair. It wasn't something I needed to know about, frankly. The first thing he did was offer to buy me something. I already had a computer and a DVD

player and clothes, so I asked for a bike. I thought it might make it easy to get around. Between the bike and the driving lessons, it cost about one point five million yen, but my father didn't bat an eye."

"Oh . . ." Karin had to work long hours to pay the electric bill. Compared to her, Shinobu seemed incredibly lucky, but Shinobu seemed very bitter about it.

"If my father had asked me to keep it secret from my mother—a secret between men—if he had said that first, I wouldn't have needed anything. But he started with the bribe, so I had to ask for something. He's the one paying for it, and if it buys him peace of mind, fine. If I'd said I didn't want anything, he never would have believed me."

Karin caught a whiff of unhappiness off Shinobu again and slowed down. She was afraid her blood would start increasing if she were too close to him.

It was hard to tell if the building had been expanded or if it had always been designed like that, but there were three towers connected with hallways, forming a C shape. Karin and Shinobu had no way of telling where Kenta was. The lights from the road barely lit the entrance of the building. They could tell that one of the doors had been left open.

Shinobu went right in. There was no light at all inside—it was pitch black. Karin stepped inside nervously, immediately freezing in her tracks. Suddenly, they heard a faint clatter, like an empty can rolling.

"That way," Shinobu directed, running down the dark hallway. He either had good instincts or night vision.

Karin could hear Shinobu's sneakers padding smoothly away from her. "W-wait . . . eek!" She stepped on a plastic bag and slipped, falling on her ass. "Owww! That hurt! Um . . . Kirioka? Where are you?" She sat up and looked around. Karin was afraid of Shinobu Kirioka, but she was more afraid of being alone in the dark. "Kirioka? D-did you go ahead?"

Listening carefully, Karin couldn't hear any footsteps. Shinobu *had* left her. He'd never wanted to bring her in the first place, so this was only natural. The wind was picking up, and she could hear it hissing through the cracks in the windows. "Eeeeeek!" She bounded upright and broke into a run. Running made the situation far more terrifying, though, because her footsteps echoed through the empty school, making it sound as though someone were chasing her. "Kirioka! Kenta! Kenta, where are you? Answer me, Kenta! Aaaaaah! Save me!"

Fear made Karin honest, and the name she was calling quickly changed. She was much too frightened to notice the irony in begging for salvation from the one she had come to save. Running on, she cried, "Kentaaaaaa!" It was so dark that she had no idea where she was going. She had run right past the staircase Shinobu had taken. When she reached a dead end, she found the door to the covered walkway was locked and had to turn back in spite of how much time she'd lose.

I have to get to the roof somehow! Karin thought. *Ah!* The faint light from the stairs provided enough visibility for her to make out a staircase ahead. She ran toward it at full speed, aiming to race straight up it—when a shadow came leaping down at her like a gust of wind. They slammed into each other. "Eeek!"

"Aiiieee!"

As the two of them fell over, Karin recognized the voice. It was Ayaha Ougimachi.

Ayaha seemed to recognize Karin's voice as well. "You're . . . Maaka? Not Shino? Fine, just get this tape off me!" Ayaha pleaded, sitting up and turning her back on Karin to show that her hands were bound behind her with tape. Her feet had been bound, as well, as evidenced by the torn edges of tape that clung to her boots.

"Wh-what is this?" asked Karin.

"I don't know! Someone called me, so I left the house—but on the way, some weird guy waved a knife in my face, tied me up with tape, put me in the trunk of his car, and drove me here! He was about to push me off the roof!"

"Eeek!" Karin gasped. It was exactly like what Shinobu had forced Michiko to confess. But that meant Michiko's brother Ryuji was wandering around somewhere with a knife. Racked with fear, Karin looked around.

Presuming how Karin felt, Ayaha added, "He went downstairs when he heard the bike. I got the tape off my feet and ran down here. If I weren't so flexible, I never would've been able to reach my ankles. That *was* Shino's bike, right?"

"Y-yeah. I came with him, but we were separated."

"*Tch,*" Ayaha scoffed. "Stupid Shino. He should've come here faster! I'm in trouble! Usui's asleep and won't wake up no matter how hard I shake him . . ."

Karin had bent down to tear the tape, but her hands froze at the mention of Kenta's name. Her voice grew shrill as she asked, "Ougimachi, you were with Kenta?"

Karin must have sounded really desperate, because Ayaha sounded slightly stunned. "Y-yeah . . ."

"Where is he?"

"On the roof."

"You left him there, with no idea when the man with a knife would come back?"

"What else could I do? He was drugged or something! I shook him and slapped him, but he wouldn't wake up. I can't carry him . . . all I could do was run."

"How horrible! I hate you!" Karin yelled as she jumped to her feet. She hadn't finished tearing the tape, but her mind was totally focused on getting to Kenta on the roof.

Ayaha's eyes widened. "Wh-where are you going?"

"The roof!"

"What are you talking about? It's dangerous! What if that man comes back? We have to get outside and call the police!"

"But what if he kills Kenta while we're doing that?" Karin's own words hit her like a brick, and tears started rolling down her cheeks. She couldn't help but think that while they were wasting time arguing, the man might be pushing Kenta off the roof.

"Maaka, stop!" Ayaha shouted, but Karin already was rounding the bend.

Ayaha was left alone. She stood still, staring up the darkened staircase, although she could no longer hear Karin's footsteps, "She's . . . serious," she uttered as her brown eyes shimmered. "Is *that* what love is?"

Shinobu quietly opened the door leading onto the roof. The school had a complicated design, with several stairways, so the staircase he had climbed was different from the one Ryuji had taken to investigate the engine noise, and different from the one Ayaha had run down after she tore through the tape around her legs. But Shinobu had no way of knowing this. He carefully surveyed the area around him, and once he was sure no one was waiting to jump out at him, he stepped out onto the roof. Someone was lying on the ground near the roof. "Aya? Oh, Usui."

It had been so dark that Shinobu couldn't tell who it was at first, but when he ran over to the body, Shinobu realized who it was and was visibly disappointed. There was a large hole opened at the base of the fence that surrounded the rooftop. Half of Kenta's body was outside the hole, resting on the twenty-inch-wide slab of concrete between the fence and the edge. His eyes were closed, and he was in a very precarious position. If he rolled over, his head would go off the edge, and gravity would drag him down.

Shinobu almost stepped on Kenta as he stuck his head through the hole and peered over the edge, checking to see if Ayaha already had fallen. Reassured, Shinobu pulled back from the hole and checked around the area again. There were scraps of torn tape on the ground, and Ayaha's purse was resting against the fence. "Aya and Usui were brought here together, but she saw her chance, tore the tape, and ran for it? Perhaps down a different staircase," he speculated aloud.

Having deliberately driven right up to the school, Shinobu had hoped that Ryuji would realize that someone had arrived and abandon the crime. But to run around in the dark shouting would make it easy for Ryuji to catch him off guard, so Shinobu had made no noise whatsoever after he entered the building. Karin had lost sight of him and made a bit of noise, but this provided a welcome distraction, and he had let her be. He'd been partially successful—Ayaha had not been thrown off the roof, and Ryuji had come downstairs. But Shinobu had not expected Ayaha to free herself and run away before he found her.

As he bent down, Shinobu realized that Kenta wasn't tied up at all—presumably because he was sleeping so soundly. Michiko must have given him a drugged cup of tea when he'd reached the Ougimachi house. "Hey, Usui, wake up!" Shinobu shouted, slapping Kenta's cheek. Kenta only moaned; his eyelids didn't so much as flutter. "You expect me to carry something this heavy? You have to be kidding. Usui. Wake up, Usui!" Shinobu grabbed Kenta's collar and pulled him upright, slapping him again and again.

"Unnnhhh," Kenta grumbled, scrunching up his face.

"Wake up right now! I have to go look for Aya! I'm in a hurry! If you don't wake up right now, I'll throw you off the roof!" Shinobu bluffed at random. But his words had given him an idea. He let go of Kenta's collar, and Kenta's head fell back outside the fence again, thumping against the concrete. Kenta groaned briefly, but he didn't wake up.

Shinobu stood up, glaring down at Kenta. *Nobody would ever know.* Kenta was unconscious. If he fell off and died, he could never tell anybody anything. Both Ayaha and Ryuji had seen Kenta half through the fence. They never would know if someone had pushed him or if Kenta had rolled over and fallen off himself. *Maybe I should push him. . . .*

Shinobu didn't like Kenta Usui. Throughout first semester, when they'd been bumping into each other in the library, Shinobu hadn't formed an opinion of Kenta. But ever since Kenta had come home with Ayaha that rainy evening, he'd been placed in the "irritating people" group.

Ayaha's fancies were constantly shifting. She was always saying that someone was cool or handsome, but her pride was so great and her fear of rejection so powerful that she never dared tell anyone she liked him. She had thrown her arms around Kenta Usui in public and told him she loved him, though.

Shinobu had figured out that Karin Maaka had something to do with the change in Ayaha's personality, and threatened her far more than any girl should have to endure, but he'd managed to get out of her that the change was temporary. That didn't change the fact that Ayaha had demonstrated affection toward Kenta, however.

When she'd gone home earlier, Ayaha had taken Kenta with her. Before, she'd always been reluctant to go up against Michiko alone and had brought Shinobu with her. *I don't like that, Usui. . . .* It wasn't because Shinobu had feelings for Ayaha. Absolutely not. She was a thoughtless, spoiled, astonishingly stupid cousin. But with her mother in and out of the hospital for years, Ayaha had lived with Shinobu a lot over the years, since they were very small. They were so close that they'd been brought up like siblings.

When Shinobu was very young, he'd come down with the mumps. His mother had made fun of him for looking strange, but Ayaha had cried, saying that she wanted to look just like him. Ayaha had believed that everything Shinobu did she could do, too. When she found out they were going to different schools, she had sobbed, wailing that she wouldn't go to kindergarten without him. Shinobu had always looked after Ayaha. His were not romantic feelings at all. That was impossible, unthinkable. Ayaha trusted Shinobu completely, and he hoped to live up to that.

Shinobu peered down at Kenta, scowling. *I'm not in love with Aya. So, why do you make me think about these things? I hate you, Usui.* All Shinobu had to do was reach out and roll Kenta over. With a little push, Kenta would plunge more than thirty feet to the cement below and die. Shinobu probably wouldn't feel any remorse at all. He had only pretended to be good for the last sixteen years, not wanting to damage his plans for the future.

Bending down again, Shinobu reached out. "Wake up, Usui." But Kenta was still unconscious. His eyes were closed, and his only response was a low groan. "You won't? Fine." Shinobu's hands grabbed Kenta's shoulders.

Kentaaa!" Karin shrieked, bursting through the doors onto the roof. The first thing she saw was Shinobu bent over next to the fence, a pair of legs lying next to him. The top half of the second person's body was on the other side of the fence, and she couldn't see who it was. But Karin knew it was Kenta—and she also instinctively knew what Shinobu was trying to do. "Stooopppp!" She ran as fast as she could across the roof, and shoved Shinobu aside with as much force as she could muster. "Stop! Don't touch him!" Karin fell to her knees, grabbed Kenta's arm, and dragged him back to her side of the fence.

Shinobu had glanced up when Karin burst through the door, and she'd seen it in his eyes. If Karin had been a second later, Kenta would have been thrown off the roof. The door Karin had flung open slowly creaked shut, creating a resounding clang. Suddenly, Karin screamed, "How could you do that? What did he ever do to you?"

Hesitantly stepping backward, Shinobu stopped and stood frozen. He didn't attempt to approach Kenta or Karin, but Karin wasn't about to let her guard down. The day before, Shinobu had shoved her into the alley with alarming speed for someone so bookish looking. Still on her knees, Karin wrapped her arms tightly around Kenta's head.

Kenta groaned, and his eyelids fluttered. "Unh . . ."

"Kenta . . . Kenta . . . hang in there!" Karin shouted. Her heart was beating violently, and she knew why. Not only had she run all the way from where she bumped into Ayaha to where she was on the roof, the realization that Shinobu was about to push Kenta off the roof had been a horrible shock. Her body and mind both were in a state of excitement, which seemed to be stimulating her blood rush. Touching Kenta was more of a trigger than anything. She had to stay ten feet away from him to avoid having her blood increase, and right now, he was resting against her with his head in her arms.

Karin could tell that her blood production systems were operating at full power. She had bitten Ayaha the morning before, but her blood vessels already were creaking. Her entire body was hot, and the heat behind her nose was particularly painful. The agony was causing tears to flow, but she wasn't about to let go of Kenta. Karin knew how Shinobu operated. She had been there when he'd threatened her and Michiko. She couldn't relax for a second.

Summoning all her courage, Karin glared at Shinobu. "Move back! Get away from Kenta!"

"Maaka, are you feeling well? You're bright red and sweating," Shinobu noted in a perfectly ordinary tone of voice.

Blood rushed to Karin's head. "Forget about me!" she snapped. That Shinobu was pretending to worry about her was infuriating. "You were about to push him off! Why? He never did anything to you!"

Shinobu had been so harsh with Karin for biting Ayaha and for changing her personality without permission, yet he had been about to kill someone. It made no sense.

"Why? I don't know. I guess if you had the chance to get rid of someone you didn't like in a situation in which no one would ever be the wiser . . ." Shinobu began to explain, as if he were talking about someone else.

Anger nearly made Karin's eyes mist over. "That's horrible!"

"Yeah, it is—but humans are very selfish creatures, and I'm more selfish than most. Otherwise, I never would've done what I did to you and Michiko."

"Shut up! That's not a reason! Kenta is . . . Kenta is!" Karin shouted, until she started to feel the vessels in her brain swelling. The world in front of her seemed to sway. She stopped breathing. *Oh no! The more worked up I get, the faster the blood rush!* Her body felt as if it were about to topple forward, so she tightened her grip on Kenta. If she let her guard down for a second and let go of Kenta, there was no telling what Shinobu would do.

Karin glared at Shinobu as her blood continued to rise. All the blood vessels in her body were swollen, and she felt so feverish that she worried she was about to catch fire. Her breathing was ragged, causing her to gasp, and her tears flowed like waterfalls. Her nose would start to bleed any second, and anxiety was preventing her from thinking straight—but she couldn't let go of Kenta.

"Unh . . ." Kenta groaned again. His eyes flickered open, indicating that his consciousness was slowly returning. "Kar . . . in?"

"Kenta? Kenta, you're awake? Hang on!" Karin cried, shaking him. Kenta wasn't fully awake, though. His eyes failed to focus. They closed again, and he fell back asleep.

"Hang on Kenta . . ." Karin sniffled.

Watching the struggling friends from a distance, Shinobu sighed. "You look really sick. Okay, I won't do anything to him. You should get to a hospital."

"I can't trust you!" wailed Karin.

"I know. But I'm not dumb enough to do anything when I have a witness—although, I suppose I could kill the witness, too."

Karin shuddered. There was nothing stopping Shinobu from shoving both her and Kenta off the roof. It would be very simple for him to make it look like an accident. But Karin couldn't leave Kenta and run away—that was unthinkable. Her heart was beating as though it could burst at any minute. Still, she remained on the roof, with Kenta in her arms, not moving.

Shinobu chuckled. "If you're that scared, why not let go of him? If you run now, you might get away. But if you try to take Kenta with you, there's no escape. Can't you figure that much out?"

"How could I ever do that? To hell with figuring things out—I could never leave Kenta here! No, keep away from him!" Karin shrieked as she saw Shinobu take a step toward them.

Karin's arms tightened, and Kenta's eyes opened. "Karin? What . . . why . . . ?"

"Kenta, don't worry! I will never . . . ever . . . !" Karin couldn't finish the sentence. She lowered her head, letting tears fall on Kenta. She could no longer tell if she was protecting him or clinging to him.

Shinobu shrugged. "Honestly . . . such a sad decision—such an emotional scene. No need to get so upset. I'm not going to do anything. I don't know who or what you have behind you, and I certainly don't want to risk pissing them off."

Karin scowled at the thought that Shinobu assumed she was part of some crime syndicate. *It's better than him finding out I'm a vampire, but still . . . ew.*

Sensing Karin's displeasure, Shinobu giggled. "Don't worry. Really, I won't do anything to him. Not for his sake, but for yours."

A look of confusion crossed Karin's face.

"Occasionally—very occasionally—I can grow to like people like you—people who never think things through. Normally, all I do is use them; however, this time, your sad determination has impressed me, and I'll abandon my plan."

Karin gathered that she was supposed to be relieved, but because Shinobu's reason for relenting was insulting, she wasn't particularly happy. And the sardonic smile on her nemesis' face only drove that home. As she observed him more closely, though, there was more to the gleam in his eyes than superiority and scorn.

"Most people I know only act according to plans and negotiations. I, especially, always think of the cost and gain, and never act according to emotion. Occasionally, I get tired of that and do something nice to people who are my complete opposite," Shinobu explained. His voice was tinged with loneliness, exactly like when he and Karin had spoken in the parking lot outside Julian.

Remembering Shinobu's family, Karin felt her heart go out to him. His mother really had wanted a girl, but had said that she loved Shinobu because he was a good boy—as though she were only able to love a boy conditionally. Shinobu's father had tried to buy his son's silence when he'd been caught cheating. As much as Shinobu might refer to himself as calculating, it made sense that his family situation would wear him out occasionally. That was why he'd described Karin's decision to protect Kenta as "emotional," because doing so put her in danger.

Karin asked nervously, "You really won't do anything to Kenta?"

"The situation is no longer what it was before you got here. If anything happens to him now, you'll suspect me, right? Usui doesn't make a big enough impact on my life for me to want to take him out with that level of risk involved. Sure, I don't like him, but I also don't really care that much. Fundamentally, I never do anything if I'm not sure I can win," Shinobu asserted logically, turning to walk toward the stairs. "He'll wake up soon enough. I'll leave him with you. I need to find Aya."

The tension drained from Karin's body. If Shinobu were gone, she didn't need to cling to Kenta protectively. She could wait for him to wake up from ten or twelve feet away, which would help her resist her blood rush. Then, she could find someone to bite after she and Kenta left the school.

Kenta blinked a bit. The soporific must have started to wear off. He lifted his head off Karin's knees and looked around blearily, murmuring, "Karin . . . ? Um . . . where . . . ?"

"Yeah, it's me. Kenta, are you awake? You're safe now." Karin let out a long, relieved sigh, and moved Kenta's head off her knees—but it was too soon to relax.

"We don't know where Michiko's brother is," Shinobu said. "After I'm gone, shut the doors. Maybe you should stick something through the handles, too."

Fear washed over Karin again. The man with the knife had gone down to check on the engine noise—but where was he now? She had completely forgotten. And Ayaha . . .

"Ah, um . . . Kirioka! I ran into Ayaha on the first floor!"

"Where'd she go?" Shinobu cried, running back toward her.

All of a sudden, the door to the stairs opened. "Shino!" Ayaha cried, stepping out onto the roof. But she wasn't alone. A man with a mustache was standing right behind her, holding a knife against her cheek.

"Don't move, brats! If you don't behave, I'll shred her face!" growled the man.

Karin gasped. It was the man she'd seen driving the car, taking Kenta away from the Ougimachi house— Michiko's brother Ryuji. He had been grinning then, but now his face was twisted with anger.

Ryuji pushed Ayaha forward along the roof.

Ayaha had managed to get the tape off her hands since Karin had last seen her, but with the sharp blade in her face, she could hardly move. The cold metal against her skin was unbearable. "Shino! Beat the shit out of him!" she shrieked. "You can do it, right? When I was in trouble before, you did a flying kick and tackled the guy's legs!"

"Aya . . . if you tell him what I can do before I try anything, the element of surprise is lost," Shinobu said, sighing.

Ryuji glared at Ayaha's cousin. "Don't try anything funny, four eyes. You take as much as a step, and her face is gone forever! Argh, where'd the other bitch come from?" he snarled, scowling at Karin.

Karin quaked. As her fear combined with her blood rush, the beating in her chest grew even faster. *Oh no, I have to get away from Kenta or I'll pass my limit!*

Ryuji was more focused on the men than on Karin. He quickly shifted his gaze to Kenta. "What? Were you . . . in that house . . . ?"

Kenta tried to push himself up, but he was still bleary from the effects of the medicine. He scrunched up his face, groaned, and collapsed back to the roof.

"K-Kenta? Are you okay?" Karin cried, quickly supporting him. *What should I do? What should I do?* She was a defective vampire and couldn't summon bats, couldn't manipulate people's minds or knock them unconscious. There was no way she could fight a man with a knife.

Ryuji snorted. He seemed to be trying to hide his own panic with a show of bluster. "Fine, the big one's still half asleep and can't do anything. I might as well kill all four of you."

"I think you'll have a little trouble making people believe four people were acting out a lovers' suicide. I can't speak for the others, but everyone knows I'm not the type to kill myself. They'll know it was faked," Shinobu insisted.

"Shut up, you little snot!"

"I'm saying this for you. Killing all of us is a major crime, and the benefits you might gain from it do not justify the risk. You really should give up."

Despite Shinobu's good intentions, getting lectured by a high school student in such a flat tone of voice was enough to infuriate anyone.

"Shut up, shut up! You say another goddamn word . . ." threatened Ryuji.

"Nooo!" Ayaha shrieked.

The knife against her cheek had pressed in.

Shinobu put his hands up, indicating surrender. "Okay! I'm sorry."

"Good. Now, four eyes, over to the fence. Not that one—stay away from the other kids. You seem like the one I need to keep an eye on. I want you by yourself."

Shinobu stepped slowly backward. Karin stayed where she was, holding Kenta up, watching.

"Right, that looks good. Put your hands behind your head, and sit down with your legs out in front of you," Ryuji demanded.

"My arms will get tired. You don't want me running, right? Mind if I lie down all the way?" asked Shinobu.

"Don't talk!" Ryuji yelled, trying to be threatening; there was fear in his voice.

It was apparent that Ayaha was thinking the same thing Karin was. "Shino . . . " One word conveyed all the tension and anxiety she was feeling.

Shinobu nodded, obeying exactly what Ryuji said. He was frowning slightly, knowing that he had no options.

Now what?

Karin's heart continued to expand violently, and she was sure it was about to burst.

Kenta was still pretty out of it. It was all he could do to sit upright.

Ayaha had a knife against her cheek.

The only person who stood a chance of doing anything was Shinobu, and Ryuji had placed him thirty feet away from everyone else.

Were they all about to die?

"Um, Karin . . . I'm a bit lost. How did we get here?" Kenta whispered. He had been drugged at the

Ougimachi house and had woken up to find himself in a very confusing situation.

"Well . . . th-that man's going to . . ." Karin almost said, "kill us," but she suddenly felt as though she were going to throw up. "Urp!"

"K-Karin?"

Karin slapped both hands over her mouth, fighting back getting sick, but the nausea wasn't going away. It was as if invisible hands were wringing out her stomach. *O-oh no! My blood's increasing all of a sudden!* It wasn't only her stomach. Her heart and veins all screamed with pain and were about to explode. All the blood in her body boiled and began to froth. *Oh god! I can't bite anyone here . . . but if my nose starts bleeding, I'll pass out! If I can't move, what will happen to me?* More important, nosebleeds were embarrassing. Karin didn't want anyone to see her like that. But the only way to avoid it was to bite someone, and the only one close enough was Kenta. *No, no, no! I can't do that! It's too embarrassing! Ugh, why is this happening all of a sudden?* She knew having Kenta in her arms was a bad idea, but until a moment before, her blood hadn't been increasing nearly as fast.

"What? Are you okay?" Karin could clearly hear Kenta's voice nearby. He was shaking the last bit of his drowsiness, and his mind was clearing at the sight of Karin's condition.

Is that why? The idea shocked Karin. Unhappy people triggered her blood rush. The degree of unhappiness, her distance from the person, and that person's mental state all could influence the speed at which her blood increased. When Kenta was panicking or angry, her blood rush was much more severe than when he was relaxed. Kenta had been asleep and fully relaxed a moment before—but now, his eyes were open, and he found himself in a strange place, with a man holding a knife to Ayaha's cheek. It was natural that he would tense up.

Kenta had no idea how long Karin had been holding him. "Karin, are you sick? Calm down . . ."

Karin had injected Ayaha with blood the previous morning. It never occurred to Kenta that she would have reached her limit again in only a day. Rather than move away from her, he moved closer, protectively.

Karin twisted, trying to get away from him. *Eeeek! Nooo . . . my veins . . . they're bursting!* It wasn't as though she'd been holding out all day, with full knowledge that she was near her limit, like she had when she'd fountained near the end of summer. She'd repeatedly denied her own condition and put off ejecting her blood. All the blood vessels in her brain had swollen, and she'd completely lost the ability to think. But this time, her blood rush wasn't affecting her mind. Instead, she could feel all the excess blood concentrating in one place—in her nose, the weakest spot in her circulatory system.

If Karin were to lose reason, she would attack whoever was closest to her, regardless of whether that person was Kenta. *Noooooo! I don't want to bite Kenta! I can't do it—it's too embarrassing!* The instincts raging through her veins suppressed reason and shame. Tears flowed down her face, and her nose burned as if fireworks were exploding inside her skull. *I can't hold it any longer!* She didn't want to be seen, but her body moved on its own, staggering forward.

Karin's oddness hardly escaped Ryuji's attention. "Hey, you there—what are you doing? Don't move, or I'll kill you!"

"Karin! What . . . ?" Kenta yelped, flustered by Ryuji's threat. Doing the exact opposite of what Karin wanted, Kenta grabbed her shoulder and pulled her back.

"Eek! Kenta, n-no!" Karin cried.

"Ugh! You don't mean . . . ?" When Kenta saw Karin's bright red face, he finally figured it out . . . far too late.

It's s-so embarrassing—they'll all see! Karin thought to herself. She couldn't speak. All she could do was focus on the sound of the blood vessels inside her nose tearing. *Noooooo!*

The sound was similar to that of a geyser bursting. Blood sprayed out of her nose, straight onto Kenta.

"Karin, wait . . . uuuuuugh!" wailed Kenta.

Shocked by the deluge of blood, everyone shrieked.

"Wh-what the . . . ?"

"Eek! Maaka!"

Nooo! Everyone's looking! Karin thought to herself in horror. Tears began pouring more forcefully from her eyes. The shocked look on everyone's face pained her.

Only one person was paying more attention to Ryuji's knife than to Karin, and realized that the knife had been removed from Ayaha's cheek amid the chaos surrounding Karin's nosebleed. "Ayaha! Attitude turn!"

"Okay!" replied Ayaha, reflexively moving her spine in reponse to the command. Her body stretched upward as she balanced on the ball of her right foot, with her left thigh parallel to the ground and her knee bent. Her right arm went up above her head, and her left arm swung out to the side, forming an elegant curve. It all took less than a second before she began to spin around.

"Argh!" Ryuji grunted, collapsing to the ground. The knife fell out of his hand and clattered onto the ground.

Karin gaped. *Wh-what? What happened? What did Ougimachi do?*

Despite the force with which she'd struck Ryuji, Ayaha had only swayed a little and remained balanced on one foot. Her eyes and mouth were open wide. She looked more surprised than anyone.

The force of Karin's nosebleed was weakening. The excess blood had been ejected, but she was becoming anemic, and her consciousness was beginning to fade out. She could still guess what had happened, though: When Ayaha was on her tiptoes, with her thigh out in front of her, her kneecap was level with Ryuji's stomach. As she turned, she'd slammed her knee into his belly.

Before Ryuji had a chance to recover, Shinobu was on him, kicking him somewhere that made him shriek. After three kicks, Ryuji's body went limp, and he lay there unconscious, like a deadman.

"He should be out for quite some time," Shinobu announced. "Aya, good work."

"Good work? Why did you suddenly call me 'Ayaha'?"

"Did you think I was your ballet instructor?" Shinobu asked, grinning. "I hoped you would. The power behind a ballet turn rivals any martial arts movement. I knew you could knock down Ryuji with one blow, distracting him long enough for me to get over here. Usui, Maaka, are you both all right?"

Karin could hear Shinobu, but her mind was so far away that it couldn't process what the words meant.

"Karin! Hey, hang on!" Kenta shouted.

Karin couldn't answer. As she collapsed into Kenta's arms, she could feel the warmth of his hands seeping into her skin—even through her clothes.

"Karin . . . Karin?" It looked as though there was red ink on Kenta's face. He stared down at Karin, his wide eyes filled with worry.

Karin's nosebleeds were always embarrassing, but getting all that blood on Kenta was particularly painful. However, it seemed her nosebleed had provided a chance to resolve the standoff. *The knife man is out, and Kirioka promised not to do anything to Kenta. We're all safe now,* she thought. Her nosebleed was painful and horribly humiliating, but neither of those things really mattered. *As long as Kenta is safe . . . I don't mind.*

Lying in Kenta's arms, Karin smiled faintly before passing out.

"You're sure you don't need an ambulance?"

"That looks like a lot of blood."

"Nah, it's not a big deal. Karin's parents told me the disease itself is being properly monitored, and regardless of whether she gets a nosebleed, it's a temporary symptom. She'll be fine again in a day or two," explained Kenta.

Karin could hear her friend's voice close by. Loss of blood had left her body temperature very low, and her back felt as though it were resting on ice. But her cheeks and chest were comfortably warm—warm and safe. She wanted to stay like this forever. She also had felt like this before. *Kenta's back!* As soon as she realized that, her entire body felt hot. Kenta was carrying her again. Embarrassed, she wanted to jump down, but her body wouldn't move. She was too anemic and couldn't manage to open her eyes.

She had never tried to measure exactly how much blood she lost with each nosebleed, but from past experience, Karin wouldn't be able to move for a full day. Sometimes, she didn't regain consciousness at all, sleeping for twenty hours straight. If someone unhappy, like Kenta, was around, her blood would increase faster, and she could recover comparatively easily. This time, only Karin's consciousness had recovered—her body was still unable to move. Her only choice was to remain in the position she was in on Kenta's back.

Karin's arms were hanging down over Kenta's chest, and every now and then, they came in contact with his wet shirt. She could smell blood on his shoulder. She knew it was from her nosebleed, and felt guilty. *Sorry, Kenta . . .*

Judging from the echo of their footsteps and the smell of the air, they were somewhere inside—probably still in the abandoned school.

"Well, if you say so, we'll leave her with you, Usui. If we call an ambulance, we'll be forced to explain what we were doing here," warned Shinobu.

"So?" Ayaha asked.

"We left Ryuji tied up on the roof, right? If they find him, that'll be trouble. We don't want to get the cops involved."

"Fine! Let the cops arrest him and Michiko. They were trying to kill me and Usui and make it look like a lovers' suicide!"

"I know how you feel, but we can't. If the media were to hear that a domestic dispute escalated to attempted murder, they'd be all over it, and your dad would be in trouble. And to find out where you were, I was pretty rough with Michiko. If she can get someone to declare that she was mentally traumatized, I'd be the one arrested. Do you want to embarrass your father and see me sent to a reformatory?"

"N-no, of course not, but . . . but that sucks! That man stuck a knife in my face, tied me up, and threw me in the trunk of a car! How can I forgive that? Usui's pissed off, too, right?"

"Well, yeah . . . but I don't really . . . I prefer not to get the cops involved," Kenta muttered.

Karin understood what Kenta meant. It wasn't that there was anything lurking in his background—but he was carrying her, and the Maaka family were vampires doing their best not to get discovered. He was trying to cover for her, which is why he couldn't work up much enthusiasm.

Ayaha muttered, disgruntled, "You too? Wuss."

"Anyway, let me handle the cleanup. Don't tell anyone about it. I'll talk with your father, and we'll figure out the best way to handle things, including whether to turn those two over to the police. If you really can't forgive him, we'll have to break his arms and legs," Shinobu suggested, smirking.

Kenta cut in. "Woah, woah, woah, Kirioka! Talk about crimes! How can you say that?"

"Just my little joke."

"Liar! A few minutes ago, when you were tying up that guy, you stamped on him and pretended your foot slipped, right? I heard a snapping noise. You broke one of his ribs, didn't you?" asked Kenta.

"Pure coincidence. I meant him no harm."

"Didn't look like that to me . . ."

"You and Maaka would prefer to avoid the police, as well, right? Seeing as we all agree on that, let me handle it."

"Okay, but it better not involve anything criminal!" insisted Ayaha.

"Yeah, yeah. So only you object, Aya. Tell you what—if you leave this up to me, I'll buy you ten parfaits at Cool Cross."

"Really?" Ayaha asked.

"I would never lie about a thing like that."

"Then fine, Shino. If you insist, I can deal."

The sound of their footsteps had changed. They had stepped off the wooden floors onto sandy concrete. The air around them came alive, blowing a breeze against Karin's skin. They had exited the school.

Karin's back was still cold, where she wasn't touching Kenta. Hit by a gust of wind, she sneezed. "Hachoo!"

"Maaka! You're awake?" Kenta asked excitedly, looking back.

Karin tried to answer, but her tongue wouldn't move correctly. "Ken . . . ta . . . sorr—"

"Never mind that. You don't have to talk. You're still anemic, aren't you? Don't try to move. We took care of everything—don't worry."

Karin could see Shinobu and Ayaha, as well. Kenta seemed worried that she would say too much, so Karin simply said, "Mm," and buried her face in Kenta's shoulder again. She hadn't noticed initially because of the smell of her own blood, but she eventually realized that Kenta smelled of earth and grass. She smelled a little sweat, too, but it was a comforting smell. *No, my heart's beating fast again . . . I hope he doesn't notice.* After shifting around a bit, Karin's eyes rested on Ayaha. The dancer's lips were pursed, and one of her eyebrows was raised grumpily—but her eyes looked less angry than forlorn.

Shinobu took a few steps toward his bike before turning back to Kenta. "Usui, you're going to take Maaka home, right?"

"Yeah," Kenta replied.

"It's awfully far to walk, isn't it? If you get on a bus dressed like that, people will notice and call the police."

"Urp!" Kenta hadn't thought of that.

Karin quickly whispered in Kenta's ear, "When Kirioka and Ougimachi are gone, use my phone and call my father." Her father Henry easily could carry both of them. Bounding lightly from rooftop to rooftop, they could get home without anyone noticing.

Kenta nodded and told Shinobu, "We'll call Maaka's family."

"Okay—and like I said, let me take care of what happened on the roof. That goes for you, as well, Maaka."

Karin nodded. Her head moved the way she wanted. She was starting to recover, and she probably didn't need Kenta to hold her anymore. "Kenta, I can stand now. Let me down."

"You sure? Say if you aren't," Kenta replied.

"I would. Really, I'm fine." Karin wasn't dizzy anymore, and Ayaha's look bothered her. Kenta let her down, but the moment her feet touched the ground, she staggered, clutching his arm.

"I knew it was too soon!" exclaimed Kenta.

"N-no, I'm fine. Where's my bag?"

"Here. We found it in the hall on the first floor."

Shinobu came back, pushing his bike. He sat down, started the engine, and called out, "Let's go, Aya. I'll let you down as soon as we get somewhere you can grab a taxi—but until then, ride with me."

Ayaha didn't answer. She stared silently at Kenta, and at how Karin was supporting herself on him. Finally, she looked Kenta directly in the eye and said, "Usui, I take back what I said yesterday morning."

"Huh?"

"I said that I was in love with you, but I take that back. You couldn't save me, after all. I don't mind being friends—but you're not fit to be anything more. I have no interest in a man who can't protect me. Because you're the one who suggested we be friends, I hardly expect you to complain."

"Uh . . . well, no . . ." Kenta stammered, utterly baffled. He didn't appear to be disappointed, but the suddenness of this turn of events took him by surprise.

As haughty as ever, Ayaha drove her point home. "From now on, we're only friends. Agreed? You may go out with whomever you like. I won't mind. Goodbye." She turned her back, taking a seat sidesaddle behind Shinobu.

Shinobu handed her the helmet. "Put this on, Aya."

"What about you?" Aya asked.

"I have only one helmet. I don't need it. Don't worry, I'm not going to crash."

While observing the cousins' conversation, Karin finally remembered that when she and Shinobu had come to the school, Shinobu had not only worn the helmet, but also had warned her that he was going to drive like a maniac and that she might fall off. This time, he had given the helmet to Ayaha and promised to drive safely. Shinobu had described himself as calculating, but confessed that he occasionally was nice to thoughtless people. He must have meant Ayaha. Karin was sure of it.

"Usui, Maaka, see you at school tomorrow," Shinobu said as he drove away, moving slowly past Karin and Kenta and through the school gates.

Karin gasped in surprise. Ayaha had the helmet on, and half her face was hidden by Shinobu's shoulder. But when the bike went by, Karin saw tears glittering on Ayaha's cheeks. *Ougimachi really did love Kenta. . . .*

When Ayaha had told Kenta to go out with whomever he wanted, her gaze had shifted from Kenta's face directly to Karin's eyes. Ayaha must have sensed Karin's feelings and given up.

Unaware of Ayaha's tears, Kenta shook his head, sighing. "I don't get her. Oh, well."

Karin felt a sharp pain in her chest. She loved Kenta and, frankly, she was glad that Ayaha had given up. It didn't make her happy, though. She knew exactly how painful it must have been, because she knew that she and Ayaha felt the same. Words spilled out of her: "Kenta . . . Ougimachi . . ."

"Mm?" Kenta asked.

". . . really loved you," Karin almost said, but she changed her mind. It was nothing but a guess, and it wasn't something she should've said aloud. In lieu of her original thought, she managed to ask, "You don't mind? If you have feelings for Ougimachi, you might be able to talk her out of it."

Kenta shook his head. "No, I'm much more comfortable keeping it at friends. Ougimachi's so random and stuck up . . . not my type at all."

"Really?"

"Yeah. And the way we were brought up—our lifestyles—they're so different. We live in different worlds. Being with her is sort of exhausting. She's a nice girl, but still."

"Oh . . . " Part of Karin was relieved, but another part of her was annoyed at how dense Kenta was. She felt sorry for Ayaha. All these feelings churned around inside her, and she let out a sigh. *Ougimachi had Kirioka with her . . . she'll be fine. No matter how he acts toward other people, he's always nice to her. I'm sure he'll comfort her.*

As Karin stood in a daze, Kenta reminded her, "Karin, shouldn't you call your father?"

"Oh, right." Karin opened her bag and rummaged around for her phone, muttering, "I just don't get it. Ougimachi's father's lover tried to kill Ougimachi for getting in the way of her marriage . . . and you get mixed up in that?"

"I don't know why, either. Michiko was the one who'd told me to come back to the house so she could thank me. She gave me some tea and sweets, and I fell asleep after a couple of sips. Kirioka says that I was probably drugged. I'd thought the tea tasted bitter, but I'd also thought that was how it was supposed to taste." Kenta was far too poor to go to a hospital very often. He'd never taken that kind of medicine, and it had worked really well. "When I woke up, I was on the roof. A man I'd never seen before was holding Ougimachi hostage, and then you had a nosebleed. Wasn't it only yesterday that you bit someone?"

"Yeah, but I was hold . . . no, um, I was too close to you," Karin replied. "We were being threatened, and I couldn't move." The truth was too embarrassing to say aloud, but Kenta appeared to buy her version.

"Oh, yeah. He did have a hostage. If you'd done anything careless, he might've stabbed Ougimachi." Kenta appeared to have been too out of it to realize that Shinobu had been about to shove him off the roof, and that Karin had desperately tried to protect him. She was relieved. If Kenta had remembered how tightly she had been holding him, she would have been too mortified to ever see him again.

The fact that I remember it is upsetting enough, thought Karin. If she hadn't been trying to save Kenta's life, she never could've done such a thing.

"Do you remember anything that happened after your nosebleed?" Kenta asked. "Ougimachi knocked the knife guy down with some sort of ballet turn."

"Mm, I saw that right before I passed out."

"After that, we tied the guy up and came down here. From what Kirioka got out of the man, I wasn't kidnapped by accident. Apparently, when I was delivering a package to the Ougimachi house, I saw Michiko selling some antiques without permission."

Michiko thought that if Kenta told Ayaha about what he saw, it all would be over for her. Michiko and her brother had teamed up to eliminate both potential witnesses—that was the truth behind it all. Kenta had no idea if she'd been selling antiques with permission or not, and although he remembered delivering to the house, he didn't remember anything that happened while he was there.

"The tell-tale heart . . . she panicked, certain that I knew, and ended up turning to crime and digging her own grave," Kenta said.

"Oh. Well, I'm glad we're all safe," Karin murmured. When she'd seen Kenta being driven away, when she'd heard that Ayaha had left him on the roof, when she'd seen Shinobu about to shove Kenta off the roof, and when the man with the knife had come out on the roof with Ayaha held hostage—all those moments still made her shudder. They were lucky to be alive.

Karin had no idea what would happen to Michiko and Ryuji, but she imagined she would never see either of them again. Shinobu Kirioka wouldn't allow it. He was relentless and scary, and Karin would prefer to avoid him in the future—but he was the ideal person to take care of a situation as complex as this. "I guess it's all over now," she sighed, relieved.

Kenta scratched his head, obviously not sharing her opinion. "We avoided being killed—but Karin, it isn't over yet. We still have the biggest problem left: the development of Akamagaoka."

"Uuuggghhh!" Karin dropped her cell phone. They still hadn't done anything about that at all. *But now that Ougimachi's retracted what she said about loving Kenta . . .* Karin worried that they might not be able to count on Ayaha's help in finding out more details about the plans. They were out of the frying pan and into the fire. Her face went pale.

Kenta glanced down at Karin, scratching his head again. "Calm down, Karin. It isn't as if the development company's going to do anything right away. For now, let's just go home, okay?"

"Y-yeah." It was Karin's fault that Ayaha had given up on Kenta and might not want to help them anymore. If she'd admitted that, her mother would be so angry. She picked up her phone, slumping her shoulders.

When they reached a main road, Shinobu stopped his bike. Ayaha got down from it, taking off the helmet.

There were a lot of cars going by, but no empty taxis.

Ayaha hung her head down, so Shinobu quietly handed her a handkerchief. She took it and wiped her cheeks. "Shino, I'm not crying because I'm sad, okay? It was windy on the bike, and something got in my eye."

"I know," Shinobu assured her.

"There's nothing to be sad about. I'm the one who got tired of Usui. I dumped him."

"Yeah, I know."

"These tears have nothing to do with that. There's something in my eye."

"Yeah, it was terribly windy."

The nicer Shinobu was, the more Ayaha's resistance wore down. She started to sob in earnest. Shinobu stood quietly next to her.

Two empty taxis went by. When Ayaha's sobs started to die down, Shinobu asked, "Did you really like Usui that much? If you still do, it isn't too late."

Ayaha shook her head. "Nah, I didn't like him like that. I didn't love him enough to run to him in spite of the fact that it was dangerous and I was scared. That's what real love is, but that wasn't what I felt. So forget it. He's not for me."

"Oh."

"And . . . with Usui, I can't go to a fancy café and have tea, and I can't go shopping. He's too busy working to go out. It'd be boring."

"True enough."

"That's why I let him go. He didn't reject me, and I didn't lose to Maaka. I simply don't like him anymore."

"I know. You made the right choice. Good for you."

Ayaha nearly burst into tears again, but she managed to keep her emotions under control. "Shino . . . you promised you'd buy me parfaits. Will you buy me some cake, too?"

"Sure."

"And not just Cool Cross. I want Ajisaiya and Rosalin Rosalin parfaits, as well. And Sky Dining at the First Hotel has an all-you-can-eat cake bar—will you take me?"

"Sure. My father gave me another payment for my silence, so I have plenty of cash."

"Silence for what?"

"If I told you, I wouldn't be silent, would I? Don't worry about it—just make a list of where you want to go."

"Okay. Thank you, Shino."

"We have to do all that starting tomorrow, though. Today, we're going straight home to take a nice hot bath and get that dirt off you, and then we're going to eat the dinner my mother has ready and go right to bed. Okay?"

"You won't come back with me?"

"Don't worry—I'll follow you all the way home. But after that, I need to go see your father. Look, there's a taxi. Driver, take her to Yamate in Natsume-chou. In you go, Aya. I'll be right behind you."

Ayaha climbed into the taxi.

Shinobu started his motorcycle's engine, glancing up at the few stars visible in the sky above. "Aya did well, so I rewarded her . . . and my reward comes from my uncle. It's perfectly natural . . . but this one will be a little expensive. How should I play it?"

The afternoon sun streaming into the corridor reflected off the aluminum sashes, dazzling everyone.

"Thank you again," Karin said, opening the door of the nurse's office and exiting into the hall. The bell was ringing, signaling the end of fourth period. *I have to get back to class and give Kenta his lunch!*

It was the day after her nosebleed, so Karin would have preferred to spend the day relaxing at home. But if she skipped school, Kenta wouldn't have a lunch. The day before, she'd been on Kenta's back for a long time, and felt as though she'd recovered. Once she arrived at school, though, she realized she wasn't in great shape. She fell over during gym in first period and had spent the rest of the morning in the nurse's office. *I wonder if Kenta's hungry . . .* Karin hadn't seen Kenta on the way in, and she had yet to speak to him. She wanted to know what happened to Michiko and Ryuji, and if he'd learned anything about the development plan.

When Karin opened the classroom door, Maki, who was eating lunch with some other girls, called out to her, "Feeling better, Karin?"

"Yeah. I thought eating lunch would be better for me than sleeping all day," Karin quipped. When she reached her seat, she removed two lunches from her bag and scanned the classroom, but there was no sign of Kenta.

"Karin, Usui is . . ."

"Eeep! Don't get the wrong idea, Maki! I'm not really . . . Kenta and I are only friends! Yesterday, he brought me home after I became anemic, and I made this to thank him!" Karin hurriedly blurted.

All the girls nodded understandingly. They all had given up on getting Karin to admit the truth. "Yeah, yeah, we know. No need to try so hard to convince us. Usui isn't here. But don't worry—it wasn't Ougimachi who came to talk to him."

"It was Kirioka—from class B. But it didn't look like a fight. It appeared as though Usui wanted to talk to him," Fukumi added.

Karin was rattled anyway. She was far more frightened of Shinobu than Ayaha. *Kirioka said he wouldn't do anything to Kenta, but just in case . . .* Carrying both lunches, she ran out of the class. She glanced through the hall window into class B, but Kenta and Shinobu weren't inside. *If they're talking about yesterday, they'll go someplace deserted . . . the roof . . . or behind the school . . .* Karin tried the roof first, but her body had so little blood that climbing the stairs took a lot out of her. She was exhausted by the time she reached the top, and took a moment to catch her breath, leaning against the door. The moment she opened the door, she heard a voice.

"So, we didn't call the cops."

Karin froze.

"Instead, my uncle paid them off . . . Ryuji's hospital bill, I mean—a mere fraction of the fortune Michiko had been after. He handed that over, they left the house, and we'll never see them again," Shinobu explained.

"You sure that's enough?" Kenta asked. "I mean, they tried to kill Ougimachi and me and make it look like a lovers' suicide. They might try something else!"

"Don't worry. He's a land developer, and in that line of work, you get to know a lot of speculators and other shady individuals. He may not display them publicly, but he has a few cards up his sleeve."

"Kirioka! You can't mean . . ."

"Don't be so grim! Did you think I meant dropping them into the ocean in a barrel of cement?"

The conversation was getting more terrifying by the moment, and Karin couldn't work up the courage to come out of hiding.

Shinobu laughed. "You ask the *yakuza* for help, and they'll demand payment two or three times. We won't do that. All a thug like Ryuji has to do is name-drop a few yakuza bosses' names, and that'll be intimidating enough. There's nothing else he can do."

"So, Ougimachi can relax."

"Well, I told her that Michiko had left, but I didn't give her any details. If you see her, don't say anything, okay? Aya is thoughtless and talks too much, so I can't tell her anything like this. You tell Maaka for me—and remind her to keep it to herself."

"Why not tell her yourself?"

"Maaka's scared of me. She'll be happier to hear it from you."

"Wait a minute, Kirioka . . . Karin is scared? Did you do something to her?"

"Nah. I'm a feminist," Kirioka claimed, unflappable. Karin's mother, who drank liars' blood, would have leapt on him in a second.

Karin put one hand on her forehead in disgust. She carefully peered through the crack in the door and saw the two boys sitting on the concrete wall, leaning against the fence.

Kenta murmured dubiously, "I find that hard to believe."

"Hmph. If you're going to be like that, I guess I won't tell you my good news," Shinobu replied.

"Good news?"

"The more upset you get, the less fun and the bigger waste of time you are, so I guess I might as well tell you—Akamagaoka is no longer the planned location for the retirement home."

"What? R-really?" Kenta exclaimed, sitting up.

Karin held her breath.

"The company had three potential locations to start with. When I talked with Aya's father yesterday, he changed his mind. One-man companies can be flexible that way. The production team must be scrambling to change the plans to the second location now."

"But why so suddenly?" Kenta asked, settling back down against the fence as his head spun. "Ougimachi said that her father's company was dealing with billions of yen, and that he couldn't change his plans simply because his daughter asked him to. Are you sure?"

"Yeah. Not even Aya could do anything with paternal affection as her only weapon. I didn't pull it off because I was his nephew—I merely warned him."

"About what?"

"That the place he'd hidden his company's secret account book was so obvious that I'd taken the liberty of transferring it to a safe place for him. For some reason, I have a knack for finding things that other people are hiding—including when I don't want to know. My uncle held out for a bit, but when I told him the new hiding place and told him a few new tricks to lower his taxes, his mood improved."

"To lower his . . . like tax eva—"

"Stop. Please, don't use such inelegant words. It's reducing taxes, that's all. If I hadn't provided that in trade, there was no way I could have pulled off a stunt like getting him to move the development site away from Akamagaoka."

"So, we won't be evicted?" Kenta asked, still half believing it.

Karin's heart pounded quickly as she waited for the answer.

"Because her father changed the location from Akamagaoka to the abandoned hospital in Sanjo-shi, your apartment and the hill itself will remain exactly as they are. Ask Aya's father's company if you want," Shinobu suggested firmly.

Oh good! Without thinking, Karin jumped for joy. *We won't be driven out! Dad, Mom, Ren, Anju . . . everyone can relax! Thank goodness! We can keep living as we have been . . . in this town, in this school . . . with Kenta.* Karin's cheeks flushed as a sweet feeling spread through her chest. She was so happy that her body was dancing on its own. *Ah, whoops! I almost dropped the lunches!* Recovering her wits, she peeked out onto the roof again, noticing that Kenta was looking really happy and was thanking Shinobu. He was very relieved not to have to leave his apartment.

"Really? That's great, Kirioka. It's all thanks to you." Suddenly, Kenta broke off. Frowning and rubbing his temples, he added, "No, wait. Two questions: What reason did you give for wanting the location changed?"

"That despite it being illegal to build a home there, there's a family of unknown nationality living there without permission? That's exactly what I didn't say. Relax," urged Shinobu.

"Sometimes, the way you put things really ticks me off."

"Your training is inadequate. All I told Aya's father was that someone I owed a favor lived there. He grunted something about helping find a new home, but he accepted it eventually. And the other question?"

"Why'd you bother?"

Karin had wondered the same thing. She was glad that Shinobu had been able to help them, but he hated Kenta. Neither of them really could be happy without knowing the reason.

Shinobu gazed up at the sky. "Half the reason is that I'm grateful to Karin for getting that nosebleed on the roof yesterday."

"What? But that's . . ."

"I'd been waiting for that knife to move away from Aya's face—but Ryuji knew I was, and never let down his guard. The longer that situation lasted, the more likely it became that Aya would become hysterical. Maaka's timing was perfect, and the geyser was spectacular enough that it gave me a chance to act. Did you know ballerinas are that strong? Every one of them can kick a tile in half."

"I understand that Karin distracted Ryuji—but what's the other half?" Kenta asked.

Shinobu's smile changed from a grin to a smirk.

Karin stiffened. She was certain she'd seen him glance in her direction. Did he know she was standing in the shadow of the doorway?

"Well, Maaka . . . hmm, I'm not sure I should tell you this . . ."

"If you don't want to say, you . . ."

"Don't sulk. I'll tell you."

The way Shinobu was beating around the bush made Karin tense. *He can't be about to tell Kenta how I put my arms around him protectively! I don't think that would be a reason for Kirioka to convince his uncle. I don't know. What could it be?*

Shinobu's smile grew even nastier. "Maaka allowed me to see her in a highly embarrassing state most people would consider unthinkable."

"K-Kirioka?"

"It was most entertaining. Maaka kept crying, 'Stop!'—but a moment later, she put her arms around me. Not an unpleasant sensation."

"Y-you bastard! What did you do to her?" Kenta roared, ready to punch Shinobu, but Shinobu easily dodged Kenta's fist, doubling over with laughter.

"Nothing! Kirioka, stop making things up!" Karin shrieked, bursting out onto the roof.

"Awesome! You got *so* mad!" laughed Shinobu.

Staggering sideways from the force of his missed swing, Kenta growled, scowling. "Wh-what? But you just said . . ."

"I meant that I saw Maaka genuinely crying. Tears and snot were all down her face. Most high school girls would never do that in front of you, right? Maaka, what do you think Usui imagined?"

Kenta's jaw dropped. Everything above his collar turned bright red.

Karin could feel her own cheeks flush.

Shinobu added, terribly amused, "She put her arms around me because she was sitting behind me on the motorcycle. There wasn't anything dirty about it, Usui. If you're going to get that mad about it, maybe you should stop pretending you're only friends and hook up!" With that, Shinobu slipped past Karin toward the door before pausing and turning back to her. "I'll make my final decision after I've observed Aya's condition a little longer—but I have far too much to do to snoop around after you two all the time. For the moment, I'm going to take you on your word. You okay with that?"

Karin nodded. She knew Shinobu meant that as long as nothing strange happened to Ayaha, he would stop trying to figure out who Karin was.

Shinobu seemed to be satisfied, but then he took things one step too far. "Now, I'll get out of the way, so the two of you can flirt as much as you want."

"Kirioka!" Kenta shouted, but Shinobu had disappeared. "Argh! Did he have to say that? 'Flirt as much as you want?' Damn!" He kicked the wall in frustration, but his expression softened when he saw the two lunches Karin was holding. "Sorry! You carried those all the way up here for me? Even though you're feeling sick enough to collapse in gym?"

"I'm fine. I just needed to rest a little longer. When I'm with you, my blood increases, so I won't be anemic for long." Karin was far too embarrassed to admit that she found it comforting to be near Kenta. She handed him the larger lunch, adding, "And I promised this."

"Thanks, really. You haven't eaten, either, so will you join me?"

"Uh . . . um . . ." Shinobu's joke about flirting echoed through Karin's head. She waved her hands around, sending her own lunch flying.

"Ugh!" Kenta yelped, vaulting into the air to catch it. His reflexes were astonishing when food was involved. "Why did you panic?" he asked as he handed the lunch back to her.

Karin blushed. "Er, um, eating together . . . I mean, Maki got the wrong idea the last time, and with what Kirioka just said . . ."

"Who cares?"

Karin's heart almost stopped. A sweet heat coursed through her body. *Then . . . maybe Kenta . . . doesn't mind if people think we're dating?*

"We both know we're only friends, so there's no reason to skulk around about it. If they want to make fun of us, let them. And if you eat here, you'll feel better, right?"

"Yeah . . ." Was that what Kenta had meant? Karin hung her head.

Kenta sat down, and he was much too preoccupied with opening the lunch to notice Karin's reaction. "Kirioka asked me to explain how the situation yesterday was handled. The cops aren't getting involved, so it appears as though we don't need to worry about anyone finding out about you. Oooh, asparagus wrapped in bacon? Lettuce and a boiled egg—rice and seaweed?"

"Sorry, I overslept and didn't have time to make anything fancy."

"What are you talking about? This is plenty. You weren't feeling well, and you still made it. I'm really grateful. Mmm, so good. Really good!"

"Er, Kenta . . . shouldn't you be chewing more?" Karin asked, sitting down next to him. As she opened her own lunch, she glanced up at the cornflower blue sky. It was the color of fall. Kenta was next to her, and they were eating together. Everything she had feared she was about to lose was safe and sound again. *We're different species. We never can be a couple, and I know Kenta doesn't think of me as anything but a friend. As long as we can be friends . . .* She could be happy.

Karin smiled at Kenta as he bit into the egg, and she started to eat her own lunch.

The rays of the autumn sun shone down upon the friends. Karin's spot next to Kenta was warm and comfortable.

Thanks to you, there are now five Karin novels.

I hardly need to write this anymore, but this novel is based on the manga *Karin* by Yuna Kagesaki, which runs in *Dragon Edge* magazine. It isn't a novelization of the manga storyline; instead, it takes place between the events of the manga. This particular novel is set early in the second term, taking place over a few days between volumes four and five of the manga.

I thought I'd been a little too mean to Karin, but Yuna Kagesaki's opinion was, "Shinobu rules! I was begging him to be meaner!"

Ohhhhhh, I could have made him go further? Dang.

Anyway, there was a phone call one day between Tokyo and Osaka that I planned to write about, but my editor suggested (or ordered—not sure which) that I stop spilling background secrets in the afterwards. So, this one's all about me.

This was a while ago, but early last winter, my microwave broke. I'd put some milk in it to warm it up, pressed the switch, and the microwave went, "*Buoooooo!*" It was such a strange noise that the cat by my feet went bolting into the other room. Apparently, the microwave was emitting loud noises instead of heat waves, because the milk had remained ice cold.

I went to the nearest electronics shop to buy a new one, intending to have it delivered—but for some reason, there was a carry cart next to the microwave section on which my eyes fixated. "If I put it on the cart and pull it, it won't be that heavy. Then, I can get the microwave home today and use it right away!"

I was an idiot. The tiny wheels on the cart did not take well to the bumpy asphalt road, and the box the microwave was in was a lot bigger than the cart itself. Every time I hit a bump, the box jumped, threatening to fall off the cart, and I would have to catch it awkwardly with my elbow. Pulling the cart left-handed made it hard to balance, so I had to pull it right-handed. Two days later, the muscle pain in my right arm had gotten so bad that I couldn't move it.

After some time had passed, my vacuum cleaner broke. I'd thought I smelled something burning while I was cleaning, but it stopped abruptly. I was very glad it didn't catch fire.

I'd ventured out to buy a new vacuum. "It's much lighter than a microwave. I should be able to carry it home myself and finish cleaning." But because I'm an idiot, I'd forgotten to take the cart with me. The vacuum might have been lighter than the microwave, but not when it had to be carried in my arms. I got home safely, though.

Because I bought my washing machine at the same time that I bought the original microwave and vacuum cleaner, I'm now fretting that it might be the next appliance to break down. When? When? I live in fear.

Let's wrap this up with some thanks:

To Yuna Kagesaki, who wrote the manga and illustrated this novel;

To my editor, Y, and all the other editors at Fujimi Mystery Bunko and *Dragon Edge,* and everyone involved with the production and sales of this novel;

And to all you readers—I thank you from the bottom of my heart!

— Tohru Kai, March 2005
Watching the news reports on all that snow . . .

Check out the following series also available from TOKYOPOP Fiction:

POP
FICTION